# honeyed fables

WHITNEY DEAN

*Dedication:*
*This book is a love letter.*

# foreword

"Why is a raven like a writing-desk? Have you guessed the riddle yet?" the Hatter said, turning to Alice again.

"No, I give it up," Alice replied. "What's the answer?"

"I haven't the slightest idea," said the Hatter.

— Lewis Carroll, Alice in Wonderland

# *introduction*

Contains themes such as grief, familial loss, heavy obligations, anxiety & panic attacks, and relinquishing control to another person for sexual pleasure.

Fallon

*fallon*

Growing up, I always dreamed of living abroad. Sitting outside a small cafe in France and flirting with gorgeous dark-haired men who spoke to me in poems and lies would be the crème de la crème way of living.

Instead, I grunt and curse as I stand on a short stepladder, pushing to the tips of my toes to reach for a large box of books on the tallest shelf. "This doesn't belong here," I mutter. Later, I would make a point to chastise Thomas, my assistant manager and best friend. If I don't die by falling off the ladder and getting crushed to death by books beforehand.

Thomas often places boxes out of my reach, so I'll finally hire someone to assist with incoming stock. But that would require me to trust someone else with tasks that I can handle just fine. At five feet four inches, tackling the constant new shipments takes away time needed for other things—like owning and managing the store. But the idea of training and learning to trust another person…

"Thomas," I croak loudly. I am itching to wipe the sweat beading my brow. My arms are shaking from the weight of the box filled to the brim with hardcovers. Even with my Pilates and cycling classes, my muscles are useless against thousands of pages.

I hear Thomas before I see him. I know he's standing in the backroom doorway, most likely smug from watching me struggle. "Fallon is capable of hard things…" he chants with a snort, enjoying the sight of me seconds away from imminent death. His teasing is always as predictable as the sunrise, but it never fails to amuse me. Except for right this second.

My platonic soulmate, Thomas O'Leary, is as beautiful as he is cruel. Okay, to be fair, he isn't evil—aside from this particular moment. He just has a strict intolerance for bull-shit toward everyone else, which always makes for exciting inspections of anyone who wants to date me. But beneath his tough exterior is a warmth to Thomas that only I can bring out.

Six-foot-something, the naturally perfect shade of ginger hair, brown eyes, and an unfair complexion of milky skin—which he keeps pristine with an impeccable skincare routine—Thomas belongs on the cover of magazines, not by my side every moment of the day. Yet, here he always is. Taunting me.

"Are you *seriously* giving me affirmations right now?" I plant my palms against the side of the box to keep it from falling on my head. "I'll fire you if you don't come here right this second…."

"And then, who will discover your body?" he interrupts while slowly dragging his feet toward me. "It'll be weeks."

I rest my forehead in the crook of my wobbling arm. "We have a constant stream of customers, Thomas. I think it'd be sooner than that. Would you please just—"

Before I finish my final plea, Thomas is beside me, his left hand planted firmly between mine on the box. "Hire someone. We can afford it."

I clench my teeth. "No."

He removes his hand, again leaving me with the entirety of the weight. "Thomas—"

"Hire. Someone."

I huff through my nose and narrow my eyes. I'm not in the best position to argue with him, though even that wouldn't usually stop me. But for the sake of my arms and life, I grit my teeth and snap, "*Fine*."

He flashes a brilliantly triumphant smile, his pearly white teeth gleaming. I hate him, yet I still find myself burying a grin as I remove my hands from the box and place my feet on solid ground. Thomas is tall enough to not require the ladder, of course. "I don't know how Ansel stands you," I mutter, leaning back against the shelf behind me.

"I'm incredible in bed," he responds quickly, effortlessly retrieving the box and balancing it against his stomach. "Why do you think he's always in such a great mood when he stops by? You should try it sometime."

I wrinkle my nose. "Experiencing you in bed?"

"Christ." He looks as repulsed as me but then shrugs. "If it'd help you loosen up, I'll take one for the team."

I roll my eyes. "Fuck off. Place those hardcovers on the 'As seen on Socials' table. They're signed, so they should sell quickly."

Thomas lifts the lid off the box, annoyingly balancing the entirety of it in one arm as if it weighs nothing. "How the fuck did you manage that?"

"I was nice." My grin turns smug. "And I met the author's agent at the book convention in Los Angeles last year. We bonded over the newest episode of *Lies, Lies, Lies*. He came to town a couple months ago, and we met for dinner. He offered to send me a box of signed copies…"

"In exchange for?"

"Prime placement on a table, of course."

Thomas raises an all-knowing eyebrow at me. "Right,

of course. Because one of the year's biggest books needs prime placement at a small bookshop in New Hampshire."

I pretend to be offended by his remark. "We were voted as the business to watch this year. Did you not see the article?"

"The one you had framed? The one hanging by the front door for *everyone* to see? Nope."

Ignoring him as he follows me out of the storeroom, my mind wanders. Because, as always, Thomas was correct in assuming that Ryan Solomon, the agent in question, wants more from me than just prime placement for his author—as evidenced by the multiple texts he's sent me and the not-so-subtle attempts at exchanging nudes. I've managed to avoid it so far. I always have an excuse for him: I'm at work, the gym, or in public. The most I've given him is a quick mirror snap of me in a two-piece set while at Pilates. He responded with a drool emoji and eggplant.

It's not that Ryan is unattractive. He is, in fact, gorgeous. He grew up in California and has the tanned surfer look about him—bright blond hair and all. And though I haven't asked for his pictures, he's sent me plenty of him shirtless. Plus, I follow him on socials. He often posts himself working out on his stories, which explains why he has so many equally beautiful women following him and commenting on his posts.

I just have no interest in being another face. Well, I'm highly competitive. Putting effort into ensuring I'm the only apple of someone's eye doesn't intrigue me. And Ryan gives the vibes of a conqueror. Once he has me, he could easily be onto the next. Perhaps I've read too many books —a hazard of the job—but I want someone who doesn't require… maintenance. If I belong to him, I expect the same in return.

"Probably why I'm single," I mutter. Thomas is used to

me often saying unfinished thoughts aloud after drifting into silence from overthinking.

Thomas drops a book onto the table with a sigh, jarring me enough to stop what I'm doing to glance at him. "You're single because you've attached yourself to this store, Fallon Madison."

I snort. When we met, Thomas was instantly drawn to the fact that I have two first names as my first *and* last names. He uses them often as if he's a parent reprimanding a child. "I'm building something, Thomas O'Leary. It's barely been a year. I'm still ironing out the kinks."

"It's time you found your own kinks, Mads."

I scowl while retrieving the empty box from the floor. "Are you implying I need ironing out?"

Thomas takes the box from my hands and nods to the front of the store as young girls enter and make a direct beeline for the Young Adult section. "I meant *in bed.*"

I lower my voice. "Your obsession with my sex life lately has reached new heights."

"Just trying to help you save money on batteries."

My jaw drops, rendered utterly speechless, as Thomas saunters to the storeroom.

Hayes

# *hayes*

I stare out the limousine window as the picturesque city of Sanderling, New Hampshire, comes into view. Known for being one of the biggest cities in New Hampshire and situated right along the coastline, the seacoast city is one of my favorites to visit. It is just a short ride away from Boston—under an hour when I ride my motorcycle.

Focusing on the historic lighthouse in the distance while sipping on beer from the cooler, I'm only half-listening to the two idiots I brought along with me. I'm still unsure how my two best friends talked themselves into tagging along on such a quick trip, even if we're rarely separated. It's partly why I'm so often in trouble with my father—even at twenty-seven years old.

Three years after graduating from Boston University, my father, Frank Fitzgerald, has finally increased the pressure on his one and only child to step up in the family business, FFJ Holdings. *It's time you learn how to become me,* he told me before I left to embark on the overnight trip to Sanderling. My father's expectations are heavy, and bringing Jace and Andrew with me is a welcome distraction from the looming responsibilities. The weight of my father's expectations and the conflict between my personal desires and the family business create a constant internal struggle.

"Fitz tapped her first," Jace says, garnering my attention. Fitz is the nickname I've had for years—longer than I can recall. Andrew awarded it to me when we were kids, but Jace quickly adopted it and never called me anything else. I'm not sure he remembers my actual name anymore.

I raise a single eyebrow in an inquiry into who Jace could be referencing. I have a roster of women I call to spend the night in my penthouse in Boston, but I rarely share women with any of my friends—especially Jace. Our friendship has always been a tangled web of competition and grudges that never seem to fade, adding a layer of complexity to our relationship.

"Raquel," Jace continues with a half-grin.

Andrew clears his throat and diverts his attention to the passing scenery, but I don't take the bait. Instead, I return my focus to the shrinking lighthouse as the limousine crosses the bridge into the city. Raquel was my favored on rotation, but she wanted more from me, and I wasn't willing to offer it to her. I wasn't aware she slept with Jace, but it makes sense. She wasn't pleased when I ended things between us, and sleeping with my best friend probably seemed like the best revenge, but it only ensured she would never be invited into my bed again.

"Remind me why we're here again," Jace says with a sigh, taking the cue to drop the subject.

"Assessment," I reply.

Jace pops the top off another beer and takes a swig. It's his third in an hour. Despite how often we partake in drinking, Jace doesn't hold his alcohol well. Allowing him to come into the small bookshop with me could do more damage if Jace acts rudely or incoherently. I don't need another one of my father's threats of losing my inheritance.

"Maybe I should visit the store alone," I continue. "It won't take long. I can meet you somewhere afterward."

"Unnecessary," Jace says. "The hottest women are always in bookstores."

"That's not what this trip is about," Andrew chimes in with a sigh. "Frank will expect an actual assessment from Hayes. This shop was voted as the best new business in the city. It's giving FFJ Holdings competition in the market."

Like me, Andrew was coerced into working for my father from a young age, as Andrew's father did before his death. We don't play huge roles in the company—we haven't honestly played *any* role thus far—but that's changing. Despite our initial lack of involvement, we both feel a strong sense of duty towards the family business.

Apparently.

Jace, however, was not offered a position at FFJ. I know that contributes to his bitterness toward me, but Jace's father does well enough on his own. He doesn't own a company but works in tech for one of the largest international cybersecurity companies. Jace's future is set.

Jace's disinterest in logic is apparent as he grins at Hayes. "Please, daddy. Let me go to the bookstore."

"Christ," I mutter, my frustration evident in my tone. Jace's playful antics, while often effective in easing tension, only serve to exacerbate my frustration at the current situation.

Andrew pinches the bridge of his nose. "That made me so uncomfortable, Jace. Please don't ever do that again."

The plea only eggs Jace on further. "Daddy Fitz, I'll be so good. I'll behave, *I promise.*"

I crack the slightest grin when Andrew starts chuckling while shaking my head. "Fuck off, Jace."

*Shoreline Scribes* is situated along a strip of shops facing the coastline, immediately giving points for the view alone. The seaside vibes of the row of stores are a massive draw for tourists.

We stare at the glass door from across the street, memorizing every detail we can and watching the steady stream of people walking inside. The bookshop is a charming one-story building with a weathered, inviting facade—like a cozy reading nook. Vintage-style stickers of classic novels adorn the frosted glass pane door, encircling the hours and operation. In the left window, a coffee bar with the newest tech in coffee machines is inviting and mouthwatering. On the right side, book spines of every color are arranged in knee-high stacks.

"The owner knows how to market," Andrew says, sliding his hands into the pockets of his slacks. "I don't enjoy reading but want to walk in, if only for the espresso alone."

"Business major," Jace adds. Even his voice carries a hint of being impressed. He points to the shops on each side of the bookstore. "Scribes stands out compared to its neighbors. It's… cozy. As a bookstore should be."

We side-eye him.

"You know I'm not wrong," he defends. "It's winter. Imagine your favorite Christmas movies. If they included a bookstore, this is exactly what it'd be like."

Andrew sighs deeply. "He's right. It's what FFJ is missing."

I read the hours posted on the door and check the time on my phone. "They open late and close early, which means it's operated by the owner and two employees at most. Frank's assistant gave me the numbers before I left, and they showed them in the green. The owner keeps costs low and outperforms a store in the Boston metro area."

"It explains why the owner wants the expansion," Andrew says.

Jace leans against the door of the limousine. "Expansion?" He looks around. "Expand to *where*?"

"The city," I answer. "That's why we're here. *Shoreline Scribes* has placed a competing bid in a new retail space in the heart of Sanderling."

"And because the owner is so heavily involved in replenishing the local economy here, Frank's bid isn't being given priority as it normally would," Andrew explains further.

Jace crosses his arms over his chest. "And he's afraid if *Shoreline Scribes* performs well in the city, the owner will start looking at Boston next. I get it."

Though Jace acts carelessly most of the time, he has moments when he reminds us that he also graduated from Boston University with a business degree. His GPA rivaled mine, though Andrew has both of us beat.

"Why not offer to buy them out?"

Andrew and I don't need to exchange a look to answer that question—FFJ can't. It isn't that the company is floundering, but since our designer gave into the minimalistic approach and gave our chain of stores a makeover, sales have plummeted. Jace is correct in that aspect—customers want the look and feel of a cozy bookstore. There seems to be a vast difference between feeling like a customer and feeling like a friend.

*Shoreline Scribes* feels like it's owned by someone who could be your best friend, and that's just from the outside. And if the owner is aware of that, approaching with an offer will show where FFJ's weakness lies.

But that isn't something we can share with Jace. FFJ Holdings doesn't fuck around with their NDAs. And even though I stand to inherit the company someday, it doesn't free me from the requirement to keep my mouth shut.

"It's being discussed," is all Andrew replies.

Jace rubs his palms together before sliding them into his jacket pockets. "Well, fuckers. I'm going inside to get a cappuccino. Maybe I'll pretend not to know how to make one, and an unsuspecting woman will assist me."

"You're an idiot if you think any woman is ever unsuspecting," Andrew says dryly as he follows Jace inside.

I, however, linger back for a moment and study the spines of the stacked books in the window. They're all classics, just like the stickers on the door. Not only that, but the books are also first editions. I recognize them without needing to open the cover. They are bent and curled at the edges, faded and discolored but pristine. The owner is either a collector or an avid reader, which means they didn't open a bookstore just because it's trendy.

An inkling lodged in my chest like a bullet tells me that the person I'm about to meet will be challenging. And there hasn't been a challenge yet that I haven't conquered.

# *hayes*

S tepping into Shoreline Scribes, I'm enveloped by the scent of espresso and old books. The comforting aroma warms me. This store could pose some serious competition for FFJ Holdings, especially if the owner wins the bid for the retail location in the city. I drag my fingertips across my forehead in frustration, sighing as I stare at the table filled with autographed copies of the year's biggest book.

Although FFJ sells prominent shelf placements to publishers—like the one responsible for the book I'm now holding, we couldn't secure signed copies due to the author's sudden surge in sales and fame.

Flipping to the title page, I curse under my breath. A signature and quote from the author mocks me. "These aren't just signed," I mutter to Andrew, who joins me at my side. "They're completely personalized."

Andrew takes another copy from the table and casually flips through the pages. "There's an entire section in the back dedicated to signed books from local authors, including some from Boston."

"This goddamn store has only been open for a year.

There are no records of the owner having any prior experience. How the hell have they secured relationships like this already?" I place the book down and look around the store, noting all the newest releases made popular by social media.

My gaze falls on a small table displaying annotated copies of various titles. A sign with colorful lettering and perfect penmanship reads "Owner's Thoughts." Only five books are available, each adorned with multiple colored tabs and notes scribbled in the margins.

"Has she added anything new?" a patron asks, scanning the table eagerly. "I've purchased three of these so far."

I raise an eyebrow. "She?"

The young woman barely notices me. "Um, yeah. Fallon? The owner?"

I didn't pay much attention to the owner's name when I reviewed the financial records, but now it's clearly lodged in my mind: Fallon Madison. I should've been more diligent and at least searched for her social profiles.

Flashing a charming smile, I ask, "This is my first time here. Can you point me toward Fallon?"

Finally, she tears her eyes from the table to look at me. Her cheeks immediately flush a bright red, and she yanks her eyes away from mine. "Su-sure, of course." Timidly, she glances around the store before pointing at an attractive man at the register. "That's Thomas, her assistant manager. He'll know where she is."

I study Thomas, feeling an unfamiliar tension in my jaw. "Are they a couple?"

She shrugs. "I don't think so. They've never overtly denied it, but I think they're just friends. He has a boyfriend." She lowers her voice to add, "But if it were me and I worked with him every day..." she clicks her tongue, leaving the implication hanging in the air.

Wordlessly, I leave her side to continue exploring the store. Andrew is doing the same nearly, covertly snapping pictures of things that could be of interest later. Jace has found a woman to listen to whatever story he's telling to hold her attention while holding a book I know he's never read.

I detach myself from being Frank's son and peruse the store as a customer would. Despite the towering book-shelves lining the walls, the store feels open and uncluttered. It isn't modern or minimalistic; it's unique. "Less is more" was clearly not Fallon's motto when designing the place, and the approach worked.

I wander to the display in the front window, curiosity getting the best of me. As I suspected, the stacked books are a collection of classics. I pick up a copy of *The Great Gatsby* from the top of a pile and thumb through the pages. Again, I mutter obscenities when the words 'First Edition' jump out at me in italics.

Since FFJ's stores are part of a chain, we don't stock rare finds like the one in my hands. Our inventory consists solely of mass-market offerings and whatever is trending.

"It's ironic to be in a bookstore when you can't read," a voice remarks beside me.

I startle and glance to my left. Standing next to me is a petite woman with bright green eyes glaring directly at me. Her hands are on her hips, and her face is etched with impatience. She is young, patronizing, and beautiful.

Irritation bubbles. "Excuse me?" I reply, not trying to mask my annoyance.

Without looking away, she tilts her head slightly toward the display, demanding I follow her gaze with a look. Sighing, I return my attention to the display and suppress a wince. Printed in bold letters on faux parchment paper, designed to match the theme of literature gone by, are the words **'DO NOT TOUCH.'**

The statement feels like another taunt.

"I would appreciate it if you return my first edition to its spot," she says.

*This* is Fallon Madison? *She's* our competition? She can't be older than twenty-five. Her ivory complexion reminds me of sweet cream and dries my mouth. My eyes drift from her long eyelashes, which peek out under her long bangs, to the slight glimpse of her left shoulder revealed by her oversized black sweater. The sweater bears her university's name in bold lettering and hangs loosely over black leggings, accentuating the slight glimpse of her curvy thighs.

Wavy black hair is a mess on top of her head, with strands poking out in every direction, yet it looks perfectly styled. And I realize a full minute has passed while I've been silently checking her out. And I'm *still* holding her book.

I didn't consider the impression I wanted to make upon meeting Fallon, but this certainly wasn't it. In fact, I wasn't sure I should meet her at all—especially since I can't reveal who I am: the son of the billionaire Boston businessman trying to outbid her.

Exasperated with my delay, Fallon takes it upon herself to retrieve the book from my hands and return it to its spot on the pile. "Would you like the name of a tutor?"

I glare. "You have quite a mouth on you."

She rolls her eyes. "Or you're just not used to being reprimanded." Her gaze wanders from my shoes to my face, disinterest evident. "I think you wandered into the wrong store. J. Crew is a few streets over."

"I know how to read," I say through clenched teeth, though I'm unsure why I need to assure her. "Curiosity overpowered the need to inspect the display for warnings, but you're the one at fault."

Fallon crosses her arms over her chest, immediately

taking a defensive stance. It's a futile effort, given that she's over half a foot shorter than me. "I'm sorry?"

"I forgive you," I reply with a smug smirk.

Her agitation with me is evident in how her mouth draws into a tight line. "Again, you seem to misunderstand."

I didn't misunderstand. I'm just enjoying irritating her. "Books like these should be behind plexiglass or in a display case, at the very least. You shouldn't have them out if you don't want people to touch them. It's too tempting."

Fallon shrugs condescendingly. "Or perhaps an adult should read the sign and have some self-control."

My stare hardens as it zeroes in on her. "Self-control isn't always possible around something so rare."

She seems undeterred by me, though I pick up on the faintest flare of her eyes. She is rare—at least in a business sense. Being as successful as she is at such a young age is impressive. Physically… well, she also seems pristine, which adds to my already cemented dislike of her.

Fallon gestures behind me with a lazy wave of her hand. "The exit is behind you."

My lips part in surprise. "Are you asking me to leave?"

To aggravate me further, she shrugs her left shoulder. "It wasn't an invitation to stay."

*fallon*

I savor the shock that ripples across the man's face. His reaction to my simple request to return my book to its proper place hinted at his discomfort with relinquishing control. I noticed him when he walked in, trailing behind the two men he arrived with. All three of them are hand- some, but the one glaring at me possesses a strikingly somber beauty. A permanent brooding expression seems etched into his features. The only time I've sensed emotion from him thus far is this moment and the one when I accused him of not being able to read.

As much as I enjoyed riling him up, my primary objec- tive now is to defend the years I've poured into collecting rare first editions of classic novels. I will not allow anyone to disrespect my collection, no matter how attractive they might be.

Yet, he stands his ground, bewildered. On the other hand, I gracefully maneuver around him and head toward the door to open it for him. But before I can do so, Thomas steps in with a smile that sparkles with amuse- ment. "Mads, what's going on? Why are you kicking customers out of our store?" Though his tone is light, the tension living in the three feet between me and the stone-cold man behind me is suffocating.

I didn't realize Thomas was watching my interaction unfold. "He… irritates me," I whisper, turning my head to glance at the perpetrator.

His eyes narrow on me in return.

Thomas, in all his teasing glory, lets out a snort. "Well, Mads, you get on my nerves sometimes, but I don't kick you out, do I?"

I scowl but can't argue. Though I might own the store on paper, Thomas has been here since it opened. It's as much his as it is mine. If he wanted to someday kick me out, I imagine he would.

"I apologize for the misunderstanding," Thomas says, but *not* to me. He gently takes hold of my shoulders and spins me around, pinning my back against his chest and holding me tightly. He must think I'm going to bolt. "Fallon is fiercely protective of her books, which makes the store run so well. Right, Mads?"

I force a slight grin and part my lips to give a faux apology, but I can't muster the strength to follow through. Instead, I gesture toward the bookshelves on the left… away from my collection. "Let Thomas know if you need anything."

Thomas sighs loudly behind me.

The man steps toward me but is stopped by a hand on his chest. His friends must've become curious about his tense interaction with me, who looks minuscule between all four men surrounding me. One of his friends extends a hand toward me. "I believe introductions will lessen the tension. I'm Andrew. I'm impressed by the selection you offer in the Non-Fiction genre. Typically, I can only find newer releases in stores. You have titles that date back decades."

I relax my shoulders and take Andrew's hand. I note

his sandy-blond hair and brown eyes against pale skin—typical for this time of year in New Hampshire. "Thank you. Most of my clientele is younger, but the tourists that stop in usually gravitate toward Non-Fiction."

With his hand still on my enemy's chest, the other friend chuckles. "I think you meant to say 'old'." He drops his hand and extends it toward me instead. "I'm Jace. You should've started with me."

Jace is *almost* as striking as the mysterious one. Tall, with dark, unkempt hair and hazel eyes, he has a dark complexion that would make him an excellent cover model for any Dark Romance novel. The only unattractive quality so far is that he seems to know how beautiful he is.

I take Jace's hand with a forced laugh, but my gaze lands directly on the nameless man. Jace notices and drops my hand to place it on his friend's shoulder. "And this charmer is Fitz."

Fitz. It's obviously a nickname—unless his parents just really admired the Boston politician.

"Fitz," I repeat, my disdain for him momentarily forgotten as we lock eyes. Fitz looks like he was drawn by a god. Black hair, ocean-blue eyes, and golden skin. Men like him just shouldn't exist. It's unfair to the rest of the world. "What a rotten crowd," I say softly, curiosity brimming. Will he understand the reference, or am I correct in assuming he hasn't read more than the price tag on an expensive pair of pants?

With a slight upturn of his mouth, Fitz nods once. "You're worth the whole damn bunch put together."

I grin. A truce. It's a fleeting moment.

I jump when the familiar voice of my delivery man returns me to the present, breaking the stare-down between me and Fitz. "No one answered the back door," Clyde says. He's an older gentleman, sweet as sugar, and too frail to move the boxes himself. I could request someone different from the delivery company, but I've grown fond of Clyde and admire his refusal to retire—despite the pressure from his management. Maybe if the store grows, I can offer Clyde a position here. I wouldn't mind seeing him every morning.

Unfortunately, Clyde's stubbornness means Thomas and I have to carry the boxes in from the truck with the assistance of our one dolly. "I forgot what day it is," I say with a sigh, glancing at the shelves behind me. The store's inventory moves so quickly that I have shipments coming every three days, with Saturdays always being the largest.

Thomas returns to the register to assist the growing line of customers waiting to check out, which leaves me to start the heavy lifting.

I return my attention to the three lingering men. "If you'll excuse me—"

"Do you need help?" Fitz inquires.

I startle at the offer. "No, but thank you. Thomas will help me when he finishes closing the store…"

Andrew gestures behind me at the lingering patrons. "That could be a while. Let us help you. It'll go much quicker with four sets of hands. Believe me, we understand you're capable of doing it alone."

He's appealing to my feminist side, which draws a small grin from me. They're trying to make it impossible for me to argue. It's valiant, really. "You're not here to help me carry in dozens of boxes. You came for the books…" I pause to lift my chin toward the small cup in Jace's hand. "And my espresso machine, apparently."

Jace tips the cup to his lips and finishes the rest in one swallow. "And look at that, I'm finished. I'm bored now." He rolls his neck and extends his arms in a dramatic show of stretching. "I think some manual labor is precisely what's needed. It's been a while."

I note the roll of Fitz's eyes before he refocuses on me. "Lead the way."

I look at each of them, contemplating. I don't relish accepting help, especially from customers, but I doubt they will ever set foot in here again. They don't seem like the leisurely, stroll-through-the-bookstore type of guys. "How many boxes are there, Clyde?"

"Twenty-four, Ms. Fallon."

I cringe. Moving even half of those sends aches through my entire body. With a slight sigh and a final act of defiance, I lock eyes with Fitz. "Your slacks might get dirty."

He quirks an eyebrow, but I swear I catch a hint of amusement. "Luckily, I heard there's a J. Crew not far from here."

*hayes*

Unlike FFJ's stores, Fallon's storeroom is bare. A few boxes left on storage shelves are full of display signs and older titles that even box stores can't sell, but I notice 'signed edition' stickers on nearly all of them. I'm desperate to inquire how she secures so many signed copies from multiple authors, but that would show I'm more interested in her store than the average customer.

I must maintain my aloof behavior, though that's proving difficult around her. She's a walking, talking argument that I'm itching to spar with at every opportunity—including the task of moving boxes, which shouldn't be a spat at all. There's only one way to do it properly—mine.

"Lightest needs to go on the top shelf," I say for possibly the tenth time since we started offloading the truck.

Fallon blows her bangs off her forehead with an exasperated breath. A sheen of sweat glistens on her brow, and for a second, I wonder how it tastes. If it's as bitter as her… or sweeter. My mouth waters, but I chalk it up to carrying boxes of paperbacks. I only know that because Fallon insists on inspecting each box before it's unloaded.

"I understand your reasoning, but I sometimes have to move them alone. It's better for me if the lightest boxes are on the lowest shelves." She points to the pronounced bottom shelf directly in front of me. "Right there would be grand."

"*Grand*," I repeat, jaw ticking. "Have you considered hiring someone so you're not reliant on just yourself?"

"Fitz," Andrew warns in a low tone. "I think she's managed quite well on her own."

"She could manage better if she delegated," I begin to argue, then stop when I catch Fallon glaring at me. That doesn't stop me. "Or, instead of stacking boxes on shelves, you could hire someone to unpack each box and stack titles instead so you can properly track inventory. You wouldn't have to search through each box when pulling more titles."

Fallon, in all her bite-sized height and stubbornness, crosses her arms over her chest. "I don't owe you reasoning for why I operate my store the way I do, but since you seem hellbent on controlling how I run my day-to-day, I will give you the simplest explanation I can."

I pick up on the condescension.

"I don't have time to unpack each box," she continues. "We close early every night to put out the new stock before the next shipment arrives three days later. And there's no point in counting inventory because I cycle through it so fast. I don't have the time…"

Again, I double down. "Then… hire someone."

Jace, having moved three boxes before finding a shelf to lean against while we continue assisting Fallon, yawns. "We could've finished by now if you'd stop arguing with her, Fitz."

Andrew shoots Jace a glare. "*We?*"

Fallon drops her arms to place her hands on her hips. "I don't want to hire someone. We're fine on our own."

I place the box I just carried in on the highest shelf. "Then I guess you won't mind if I put this here," I say.

Andrew pinches the bridge of his nose. "Fitz…"

Fallon's lips part as heat fills her cheeks. I can tell by the way her skin reddened. "Did you walk into my store today with the specific task of being a jackass?"

"That's just Fitz," Jace pipes in.

Ignoring us, Fallon storms out of the storeroom and hikes up the small ramp into the truck bed. Only a handful of boxes remain, and none she can move herself, so she's trying to distance herself from me.

I follow her, crouching slightly since I'm too tall to stand erect. Fallon, however, still has inches between the top of her head and the truck's roof. I palm the truck's exterior and duck my head to watch her pace. My presence has clearly annoyed her.

I say nothing. I just watch, slightly amused by her antics. She has her hands on her hips, muttering insults under her breath as if I can't hear her. Sweat glistens on her temple and slowly drips down her cheek. My grip tightens on the cool metal of the truck, but I'm not convinced the shiver retreating down my spine isn't from something else.

From my little time with her, I've gathered that she doesn't hand over control easily. It's apparent in the way she carries herself. I haven't seen her relax since stepping foot in her store an hour ago. I could relieve that for her if I didn't find her so irritating.

"Don't just stand there," she bites, whipping her head toward me. She gestures toward the remaining boxes. "I'll compensate you for your help today."

I lift an eyebrow. If she only knew how deep my pockets run. "We offered to help, Fallon. We're not expecting payment."

Defiance squares her shoulders. "I don't want to owe you anything."

I drop my head with a chuckle. "Believe me, you wouldn't be able to afford what I'd ask of you."

Curiosity swims in her eyes. And a little bit of pride. She could pay us something if she genuinely wanted to, and she might still try to prove that her store performs well. But that's not why she's silently staring at me. She's searching for what I could mean.

"And what…" She clears her throat. "What would that be?"

Grinning, I lazily lift my left shoulder in a shrug. "As I said, you couldn't provide it."

She squares her shoulders. "I can afford it…"

"I'm not interested in your money, Fallon."

What am I doing? I can't be interested in acquiring *anything* from her. This is a dangerous game I'm stepping into, but her obstinance is begging to be broken. Her mind needs a break from the constant overthinking.

She pulls the corner of her bottom lip between her teeth, her head tilting slightly to the right. The heat in the bed of the truck is adding to the tension, causing my dick to swell from the movement of her mouth. And she seems to feel the same pull as me when she lifts her hand to wrap around the column of her throat. She's thirsty.

My mind swims into a dark abyss. As curious as she might be, approaching her with a simple, 'I could fuck the tension right out of you' wouldn't work with someone like her. She would need convincing. She'd be…. a challenge.

At the very least, staying near her would help us monitor her store and her progress in acquiring the city location. I could get under her skin.

But the words, "Hire me," slip out of my mouth long before I fully commit to this idea.

She stalls. She literally seems to just… time out. Her

lips part, her pupils widen, and her head tilts in confusion after half a minute passes by. "Uh, what?"

I have to seem confident in this impulsive idea of mine now, or she won't even consider it. "I just moved here from Boston. I was planning to look for jobs today. I have experience in retail." That is not a complete lie. We own hundreds of store locations across the United States. "I can help with shipments. Hire me."

She's going to say no. Nothing about me appeals to her, especially after her first impression of me. But she doesn't speak up—the male voice behind me does. "Done. Can you start tomorrow? I'll train you myself."

Fallon whips her head to glance behind me, her eyes narrowing on Thomas, who snuck up on us. Andrew and Jace are a pace behind him, staring at me in confusion. I shake my head slightly, silently imploring them not to say a word. "Tomorrow," I say, buying myself a few seconds to devise an excuse. "I'm moving into my apartment."

"Wait a second—" Fallon starts to say.

"No problem," Thomas interrupts. "Our next shipment comes in three days. How does that sound?"

Three days will buy me time to try and sell this idea to my father and secure a place to live. But I don't look at Thomas to confirm. Instead, I lock eyes with Fallon and promise, "I'll be here."

*fallon*

A s the store closes and it's just Thomas and me, a detectable tension fills the air. He's been avoiding me since Fitz & crew left, but I know he can't keep it up forever. I drum my fingers against the counter, watching him close out the registers impatiently. A smirk plays on the corner of his mouth, but he continues his silent treatment, adding to the growing tension.

Finally, I break. "Thomas, what the fuck?"

He doesn't even pause counting. "What?"

"What?" I repeat. "What?!"

"You said you'd hire someone this morning," he explains far too calmly for my liking. "I was just speeding up the process. He offered, Mads. Whether you like him or not is irrelevant. We need someone now."

"I could've interviewed someone from the dozens of applications I receive every week," I argue. "You didn't even give me a chance—"

"Because you wouldn't have done it," he interrupts, powering down the iPad and finally turning to face me. "You would've continued finding excuses not to do it."

I bite my tongue. Literally. Because he isn't wrong.

That's precisely what I was planning to do. "I don't like him."

"Noted." He places his hands on my shoulders and dips his chin to hold my eyes with his. "If he's a problem, I'll get rid of him immediately. Scout's honor. But you owe me a drink if he isn't and proves useful."

I turn my head away, but he grabs my chin gently and pulls it back. "Fallon, we're growing too quickly to continue running this store ourselves. I would sweat blood for this store seven days a week, and so would you. But it doesn't mean we should. It's okay to take a breath. We're in this together, remember?" His words, a testament to our shared commitment and personal growth, resonate in the air.

I want to argue more than I want to take my next breath, but the logical side of me—the one I keep buried down deep—knows he's right. We haven't had a break since we opened. For our sanity, I suppose I could tolerate Fitz on the days we have deliveries. How bad could he indeed be?

"He's on probation," I lament, keeping my defiant side in check. "He doesn't have three strikes, Thomas. He has one."

Thomas squeezes my shoulders. "Understood. Now, let's go get some food. You're far too *hangry*."

I open my mouth to retort, but my stomach chooses to growl this second. Traitorous bitch. "*Fine*. But I get to choose."

Thomas gaslit me into thinking my idea was the Mexican food we had for dinner. I don't know how my asking for somewhere with a fat, juicy steak ended with us meeting Ansel at *Huerta*, but I can't complain when chips and salsa are involved. But at this moment, I have never felt more bloated, which is how I ended up at the Pilates studio for the late-night class.

I always attend the five am class, but today's exertion of mental energy and frustration has me wound up too tight. And since I have no man on rotation and only my trusty vibrator available for an orgasmic release, I figured I'd try something different tonight that doesn't require me to think about our latest hire and how I'll handle him moving forward.

Of course, that would be much easier if he wasn't walking out of the liquor store next to the Pilates studio the moment class finishes. Immediately, I become aware of the very little I'm wearing and how disgusting I must look with my hair stuck to my face and neck from the sweat.

Maybe he won't see me if I just turn—

"Fallon."

He doesn't say my name like a question. He says it like he'd recognize me anywhere, even after only spending an hour with me. He's changed since he left the store earlier and is in much more casual attire. Less prep, more athleisure, and I can't help but notice how attractive he is —especially when I look like *this*. It's an unexpected connection, one that leaves me feeling intrigued and a little off-balance.

"Fitz," I reply, prying my wet bangs off my forehead.

He glances at the door I just came out of, then drags his gaze back to me, undoubtedly noting my attire. I guess this isn't a great impression of the woman who's supposed to be his boss. He's seen more of me than any man has in a long time. My hot pink sports bra and black spandex shorts don't exactly hide much. "Pilates," I say, like he can't read the name on the door. That's twice I've implied he can't read.

"You're not cold?" he asks.

I should be. It's nearly freezing, but I always exert so much energy in class that I don't notice the temperature until the adrenaline dies. Bumping into him has jump-started my heart and will keep me warm for at least another five minutes. "I don't live far," I explain. "By the time I walk home, I will be."

He lazily gestures toward the parking lot. "Let's go. I have a car. I'll take you home."

I shake my head. "It's only two blocks…"

"It wasn't a question." Without room for argument, he starts toward the parking lot and doesn't look behind him to see if I'm following.

I am. I don't know why.

He leads me to a sleek 2-door coupe and opens my door, giving me no opportunity to turn down his offer. But before I slide in, I note the sticker on the window. "Rental?"

He waits to reply until he's beside me. "For going back and forth between here and Boston. I haven't moved everything yet. I ride a motorcycle, which doesn't hold room for boxes."

*Of course, he does.*

I drum my fingers against my knees and stare out the window. We'll only be in the car for five minutes. We don't need to fill an awkward silence as short as that, right? The leather seats are not ideal for a creature as sweaty as me, and I'm hesitant to lean back and get comfortable. With my luck, I'll get stuck, and he'll have to pry me off.

"So… you're from Boston." I'm not great with lulls in conversations. Maybe it's because I was an only child and would get so lonely that I always chatted with my stuffed animals and dolls while growing up. Or perhaps it's the pressure of needing to ensure the other person is having a decent time with me. Not that Fitz being content should matter.

"Yes," he replies.

One-worded answers are the bane of my existence. How do I keep a conversation going when you give me the bare minimum? "I visit often. I love how fast-paced and lazy it can be, depending on where you go. Of course, it's my favorite during Autumn…."

I drift off when we stop at a light, and he asks, "Can you tell me where to take you?"

My cheeks redden. Sharing where I live is an important step in ending this awkward interaction. "Right…" When he flips the right blinker on, I snort. "No, I mean… right, as in… anyway, make a left at the next light. My building is the second one on the street."

We say nothing else to one another. He follows my directions perfectly, pulls right next to the curb, and places the car in park before exiting. I blink, confused. Is he expecting an invitation inside? I don't have much to offer unless he's in the mood for protein shakes or an assortment of fruit. I should really carve out time to pick up some groceries.

When my door pops open, I startle and stare at him. Did he just… get out to open the door for me? A man hasn't done that for me since I lived at home. My dad always opened doors for my mom and me. He said I shouldn't date a man who doesn't open doors for their significant others.

"Um, thank you," I murmur, stepping outside and shivering as the cold air bites my bare skin. "And thank you for the ride home. I suppose it's colder than I thought."

He nods in reply, closing the car door behind me.

Fitz is not a man of many words.

I clear my throat and nearly trip over the curb as I step up. "So, I'll just see you at the store then?"

He circles the car and leans against the driver's side door. Even when he's not at full height, a noticeable difference lives between us. I feel miniature beside him. And he's realized it by the way he stares at me—like he could pick me up and place me in his pocket if he wanted. "Will you?" he asks with slight amusement. "I figured you'd find a way to talk yourself out of letting me return."

I crack a small smile. "I still could."

After sliding his hands into the pockets of his sweatpants, he lifts a shoulder in a lazy shrug. "I'm cheaper than you'd spend hiring security to escort me out."

I raise an eyebrow. "Are you saying you wouldn't leave willingly?"

For the first time since I met him, Fitz chuckles. The sound widens my smile. "I rarely do anything I'm asked."

My expression conveys faux surprise. "Really? I hadn't noticed that at all. You seem so… easy to get along with."

"You're in for some surprises then, boss." He lifts his chin toward my door. "Head inside before you catch a cold. I doubt you want to leave the store to Thomas and me."

That thought alone causes me to cringe, and I step closer to the door. "I hate to admit you're right." Before I punch in the security code on the pin pad, I throw him a look over my shoulder. "Goodnight, Fitz."

He doesn't return the sentiment, but I pause when I arrive at my apartment and glance out the window that overlooks the street. Fitz is staring directly at me, the corner of his mouth tugging in the smuggest smirk I've ever witnessed before he slips into his car and disappears into the night.

And I forget how to breathe.

*hayes*

I don't know why Andrew and Jace insisted on supervising the movers with me. It's been two days since we met Fallon, and neither has broached the elephant in the room. We didn't talk about it on the way back to Boston yesterday and ignored it at dinner last night —most likely because we were out with other friends—but now, I brace myself for the inevitable line of questioning.

It's fair since I've taken up residence in a different state, though nothing will change. I'll still commute back and forth every week. My father's reaction to my initiative to watch over Fallon's store closely was unexpected. It's the first time he's been impressed by anything I've done in a while. Granted, I didn't receive more than strict instructions on what to report back, but it wasn't another lecture on when I would finally step up for the company.

My mother is at a spa in South Florida, but the furniture set up at my new condo reeks of her taste. There's nothing she does better than spending money on needless things. And in her unique way, it's how she still tries to be involved in my life. It hasn't been a secret that my father has mistresses. Despite this, my mother won't leave him.

She copes by surrounding herself with everything she could ever want, and my father will continue giving her exactly what she asks to keep her from asking him too many questions. It's unhealthy, but it's worked for them.

It hasn't given me the best outlook on relationships.

Jace sits on the couch and props his feet up on the marble coffee table, his beer bottle hanging loosely from his left hand. '*My housewarming gift*,' he'd said when he brought two sacks of liquor and beer. Neither Andrew nor I have joined him yet, but instead, I settled for glasses of the sparkling water Andrew brought.

The luxury condo I've rented is nearly 2,000 square feet and overlooks the water. The empty lighthouse is easily visible from my balcony, which was the biggest draw to renting this place. And even though it's fucking freezing outside, a few sailboats are littered across the water. I have an extra bedroom and bathroom, which I'm positive will be used frequently by Jace—given that his overnight bag is already sitting on the new bed.

"If Fallon ever comes over, she's going to wonder why the fuck you asked for a job," Jace calls out, ensuring I hear him from where I've gone to stand on the balcony.

That thought has crossed my mind, too. The building Fallon lives in doesn't have residences this size. I've already examined her building's floor plans and memorized her address. "She has no reason to be here," I reply, keeping my voice at a normal volume. He can walk outside if he wants to have a conversation.

Andrew leans against the balcony wall opposite me. "I understand why you did it," he begins, placing his glass on the ledge. "But I don't know how you'll be able to keep up the facade. You're the only son of a Boston business tycoon."

I finish my drink and silently watch the jagged waves wash over the rocks surrounding the lighthouse. The rough nature against the tranquil structure reminds me of Fallon. I want to test the waters with her. I want to know how long she can fight me before she can no longer resist the pressure.

"Fallon is too invested in Sanderling to know who I am," I state. "Until she's ready to expand into the Boston area, we don't need to worry about her finding out who I am."

"You might be underestimating her." Andrew crosses his arms over his chest. "I don't find her naive."

"She isn't," I confirm. "Not in the business sense."

From the corner of my eye, I see Andrew shaking his head. "No, Hayes. Nothing can happen with her."

I know the risk I'd take if I let my curiosity about her get the best of me. Mixing business with pleasure never works, especially when she can't know who I am. But I need to know who she is if we want to properly control the competition and prevent her from expanding.

"Can't really blame him," Jace remarks after joining us on the balcony. The beer bottle he was working on has been replaced by a new one. "But she's not your type, man."

Unfortunately, he's right. Women from my past have always tried to seem stubborn and hard to manage, but I knew it was an act. They wanted to argue with me only to be controlled in the bedroom. Fallon genuinely seems *difficult*. Taming her wouldn't be as simple as tying her to the headboard and fucking her until she's limp in my arms. She needs to be… nurtured. Understood. Heard. And, like me, she wants everything done *her* way.

We're fire and ice. Conversations with her have been like trying to drown in shallow water. Not impossible, but not fucking simple either. Yet, I'm drawn to wanting more.

This is why I find myself outside Fallon's Pilates studio after leaving Jace and Andrew at my condo. I will see her for my first day at Shoreline Scribes tomorrow, but I want to learn her habits and schedule—what makes her tick. Running into her last night wasn't an accident. I saw her leaving her store after work, the frustration from our earlier encounter in how she moved her body. Tension seems to have a permanent residence in her muscles, but she was looser last night. Relaxed. Covered in sweat. Despite the cold, I couldn't stop imagining how warm her skin must've felt.

I lean against my rental and slide my hands into my pockets. Fallon is inside, talking to her male instructor. She's telling him something, and his responding smile is far too broad. Instead of shorts, she's in high-waisted leggings that accentuate the mesmerizing flare of her hips. She has the hood of her gray cropped jacket pulled over her head, her messy ponytail sticking out of it to rest against her chest.

I'm so fixated on her that I don't realize I'm no longer alone until Jace speaks. "See something you like?"

"Fuck," I mutter, dragging my hand down my face. I don't need to look at Andrew to know he's judging me harshly. He's known me too long to not realize what I'm doing. "The fuck are you two doing here? You aren't the ones who moved."

"You're out of beer," Jace replies, placing his hand on the hood of the car and continuing to watch Fallon with me.

I clench my jaw. If Jace realizes my interest in her extends past gathering intel for the company, he'll see her as another competitive challenge. "I came here to pick up a burger for lunch." I gesture toward the restaurant attached to the studio, opposite the liquor store on the other side. "I guess Fallon takes Pilates and cycles here."

"Great. Let's go inside and eat then," Andrew suggests dryly.

My gaze flickers back to Fallon, still speaking to the man inside. They're laughing together while she bounces back and forth on the balls of her feet. It's the loosest I've seen her. Apparently, when she's genuinely distracted by something, like a decent conversation, she's lighter. Joyful, even.

What thoughts plague her in the silence?

*fallon*

I tap my fingers against the counter, unable to stop watching the door. Today is Fitz's first day working at the store. I haven't seen him since he dropped me off at my apartment the night I bumped into him. I'm half-expecting him not to show, but I fear he's just stubborn enough to prove me wrong. My attempts to look for him on socials were unsuccessful. It would've helped had I asked his last name, but Thomas hired him so quickly that none of the necessary paperwork for a new hire was filled out. The mystery of his sudden appearance adds to the tension in the air.

"He could be a wanted felon," I say, checking the time on my phone. "We could be harboring a fugitive."

"He's not moving in here," Thomas replies dryly.

It doesn't matter what the reason is I craft it in my mind. Thomas isn't going to budge. He's convinced we need help, and I agreed to give Fitz a chance. But that doesn't settle the gnawing in the pit of my stomach. Something about him triggers my fight or flight. I want to know more about him while putting on my tennis shoes so I can run as far away as possible. "Okay, but the moment he does something wrong…"

"He's out on his ass," Thomas finishes. "Would you just breathe? Go in the back if you're going to have a meltdown."

My eyes narrow into a glare. I have a retort geared up and ready to go, but the sound of the door opening gives me pause. I can *feel* him before I see him. My heart starts to race, and I can feel a bead of sweat forming on my forehead. Without turning my head, I know he's looking at me. His presence is heavy, as if each step tightens the air around me until I can't breathe—like he would need to give me each next breath.

"Good morning, Fitz." Thomas nudges me in the ribs with his elbow. "Fallon just told me how excited she is that you're joining us."

"Is that so?" Fitz's voice, coated with honeyed sarcasm, drips down my spine. "I'd love to hear that directly from her."

*Look at him*, you imbecile. I'm suddenly aware of everything I'm wearing. How my hair is styled. If my breath smells okay or if I should've skipped the coffee this morning. I did keep my outfit overly simple this morning once I realized I was standing in my closet for half an hour, wondering what I should wear for his first day. I regret the lapse in judgment when choosing straight-leg jeans and a long-sleeved black tee.

When I turn my head to greet him, I choke back my words. He's in a loose, chambray button-down shirt, the top two buttons left undone to expose a smooth chest, and a fitted pair of slacks. A puffer jacket is draped over his arm. He looks like he just stepped out of a magazine or off a yacht. His hair is slicked back, his face cleanly shaven, and his shit-eating grin staring back at me.

"Did you order the entire catalog?" I ask, referencing my few-days-earlier dig at his J. Crew wardrobe.

"Unbelievable," Thomas mutters.

Without missing a beat, Fitz spins in a slow circle and extends his arms out to the side, giving us a full view. "I wanted to look exceptionally nice for my first day working with you, Fallon." He pauses to widen his grin. "Your standards seem impossibly high to meet."

*Oh.*

Thomas snorts before leaving me standing there alone with the man who just (teasingly?) insulted me—probably to avoid witnessing a murder. I might soon become a fugitive.

I gather my hair in my hands and put it in a bun on top of my head. A nervous habit, though I suppose it could seem like I'm readying for a physical throwdown with the giant standing before me. "You're lucky there's a counter between us," I say, patting the countertop.

Fitz's head tilts slightly. "You're the lucky one, Fallon."

My mind spirals, searching for the meaning behind those words. I've read too many books since I immediately imagined him throwing me across one. Why did he have to walk into the store looking like this? He's like an untouchable tease. My time with him needs to be spent convincing myself that a man this beautiful cannot be good in bed.

Maybe Thomas was right. Perhaps I do need to look outside my trusty vibrator for release because working with Fitz will only worsen the physical ache. "Do you have a girlfriend?" I blurt out, my eyes widening after the words leave my mouth. My mother's lessons about thinking before I speak went right out the window.

Fitz drapes his jacket across the counter, seemingly buying time before he gives me an answer. I could take it back. *Never mind, ignore my attempt to pry into your personal life. Spare me the humiliation.* Whichever answer he gives me won't be satisfying. If he does have a girlfriend, I'll always wonder about her and wait for her to drop by the store. I'll have to watch them interact and be *so cutesy, so demure*.

If he doesn't have a girlfriend, then…

"No," he answers after a minute has passed.

He doesn't give me anything else. I mean, 'no' is a complete sentence and doesn't require an explanation, but it still leaves me wondering why it took him so long to answer. Is it complicated with someone? Has he had his heart broken?

"Me either," I say unnecessarily. "A boyfriend, I mean. Unless you count this store. I'm basically married to it…"

I drift off when Fitz circles around the counter and stands beside me. His commanding presence makes me fight the urge to shrink. I don't cower. I raise my chin and hold his stare despite my stomach turning jelly from how his icy blue eyes hold mine. "No?" he repeats, questioning. "A customer seemed to think something was happening between you and Thomas."

I can't hold back my laughter and a partial cringe. "Me and Thomas? No. God. We'd kill one another. He has a boyfriend, anyway. Not that it'd matter if he didn't." I blow out a deep breath to rein in the rambling. "Thomas is my best friend. He's like a brother to me." Then, I have a question of my own. "Wait… did you ask someone if we were together?"

The corner of Fitz's mouth barely twists, and he evades my question by tapping his knuckles on his jacket, still lying across the counter. "Where would you like me to put this?"

His communication could use some work.

Thomas reappears from the backroom at the perfect moment. "I need to stay up front since we're about to open, but Thomas will show you and explain the delivery schedules. We won't receive any new stock until later this afternoon, so you can spend the morning getting acclimated if you'd like. I'll have paperwork for you to fill out later."

Fitz grabs his jacket, then pauses. "Paperwork?"

I power on the iPads we use for checkout. "New hire paperwork. It won't be too much. I'm guessing Fitz is a nickname? I can continue calling you that, or I'll use the name you write down. It's up to you."

"Don't tell me your name is Fitzgerald Grant," Thomas says upon approach. "I miss *Scandal*. Mads and I binged it on Netflix not long ago. Olivia Pope? GOAT."

Fitz's confused expression makes me grin. "It's a show that isn't on anymore," I explain. "Is that your name, though? Fitzgerald Grant?"

"Fitz is a nickname, and that's what you can continue to call me." He gestures toward the backroom. "Lead the way."

---

Hours pass before Fitz emerges from the backroom. The morning rush has just settled, and I'm returning books to shelves from customers who changed their minds at the last minute when they realized just how large their piles had gotten. I didn't forget he was here, but my mind is elsewhere when he appears behind me and makes me jump out of my skin.

"*Fuck*," I mumble, clutching the fabric of my tee between my fingers. "You're a stealthy motherfucker."

With a chuckle, he leans against the adjacent shelf. "Hearing words like that come out of your mouth is surprising."

I loosen my hold on my shirt as my heartbeat slowly returns to normal. "It's a habit I've been trying to break." The stacks of rare classic novels are visible from where we're standing, and when he motions toward them, I can't help but grin. "Not getting another itch to touch them, are you?"

His eyes dance with amusement. "How long have you been collecting rare editions?"

I hum in thought, thinking back to when my very expensive hobby started. "I studied Literature in college, but my love for the classics started when I was young." I continue shelving books from the pile in my arms. "There was a fair when I was ten. My mom pulled me out of school to take me with her. One of the booths was full of books."

I turn to face him after I finish putting the books away and slide my hands into the back pockets of my jeans. "I hadn't read classic novels yet. I had just finished the *Harry Potter* series. My mom struck up a conversation with the owner while I wandered around. I knocked over a tall stack of books." I can't help but laugh at the irony. "And that's when I saw an edition of *Little Women*. The edges were torn, but the pages were readable. And I promised my mom that I'd finish all my chores if she could lend me the $45 to purchase it."

By the time I finish telling the story, Fitz is smiling. "And is that edition included over there?"

I nod proudly. "It is."

His smile softens. "I'd love to see it."

The request falls over me like silk. "It'd be my pleasure."

*hayes*

After arriving at my new apartment after work, I wasn't surprised to find Andrew waiting for me. We haven't talked much yet. He's been on calls ever since arriving. I anticipate he won't be too pleased about what I need to tell him.

I lean back in my chair, the coolness of the leather against my skin grounding me in the moment. Andrew sits across from me, fiddling with his phone. Fortunately, he kept the trip secret, giving us time to talk without Jace nearby.

"Alright, so what's going on?" he asks without looking up. "How was your first day working with Fallon?"

I run a hand through my hair, setting a glass of water down on the table. "I used your last name and Social Security number on the new hire paperwork," I say, trying to sound casual about it.

Andrew finally looks up, his brow furrowing as his gaze locks onto mine. "Wait. You did what?"

I sigh, feeling the weight of the situation settling in my chest. "I know, I know. It's... not ideal. But I can't have

Fallon knowing who I am. Not yet, anyway. If she does, it'll be game over before the fun starts."

Andrew leans back, clearly taken aback. "And you think this is the best way to go about it? Pretend to be someone else? What if she figures it out?"

I see the disapproval in his eyes, and it stings a little. But I'm not about to back down. "I didn't have much of a choice. I can't exactly reveal my identity just yet. Not when my father's already set his sights on taking her business down."

Andrew is quiet for a long moment, his expression unreadable. Finally, he mutters, "This isn't going to end well, you know."

"I know," I say, but I can't bring myself to regret the decision. Not yet, anyway.

My phone buzzes on the table, and I pick it up without thinking. It's a text from Thomas. He must've grabbed my number from the paperwork—one of the only true things I wrote down. And I can't help but wonder if maybe Fallon added me to her contacts, too. Or why she isn't the one texting me.

Fitz, I'll deny I ever told you this.

Fallon is working late tonight and might need help with inventory. One of the shipments got fucked up and came in tonight instead.

I'd help, but Ansel is sick with the flu. I might not be in tomorrow.

Secret is safe with me.

On my way.

Thank you, President Grant.

I can't help but smirk. "Speak of the devil. I'm being beckoned."

Andrew raises an eyebrow. "You're going back there tonight?"

I pause for a moment, weighing my options. "Yeah, she needs me. And it's an opportunity to learn more about her. Go to Boston, Andrew. Come back this weekend."

Andrew shoots me a look of disbelief but doesn't say anything more. Instead, he stands and grabs his jacket. "Fine. But don't say I didn't warn you."

---

Later that evening, I'm walking down the aisles of Shoreline Scribes. The warm, familiar scent of coffee and old books envelops me. Fallon is at the register, ringing up a couple of customers. Her attention is entirely on them, and I make sure to keep my presence low-key as I approach the back.

I stay silent until she wraps up what she's doing, content to watch her as she powers down the iPads and locks the front door. "Is everything okay?" I ask as she approaches, leaning against the doorframe of the stockroom.

She glances up from her phone, her face lighting up slightly at seeing me. "Fitz," she says, her voice a little surprised but not unwelcoming. "Thomas called you, didn't he?"

I grin slightly. "I plead the fifth. I'm here to help, Fallon. You should've called me."

She tightens the bun on her head, though it does nothing to calm the wild strays. "I don't have your number."

That answers my question. She didn't pull it from the paperwork. "Hand me your phone," I demand gently.

She hands it over without hesitation. With a chuckle, I flip it around and hold it in front of her face to unlock it. Her cheeks flush, but she smiles as she watches me input my name and number into her contacts. "You have no excuse now, Fallon. If you need me, day or night, you call me. Deal?"

She slips her phone into the back pocket of her jeans and studies me for a few seconds. Her earlier look of surprise lingers, but it's mingled with something more now. Understanding, maybe. "I promise."

"Great. Now, show me these unwelcome boxes." I take a step back to enter the storeroom, and she follows. "Do your shipments often switch like this? Do I need to plan unscheduled deliveries for my nights?"

That draws a small laugh from her. "Never say never… but no, never. This is the first time it's ever happened, which means I'll have too many of something and might need to cancel a future delivery of a title."

I start opening the boxes. "Nah. You seem to move inventory quickly enough. I'd be more concerned about shelf space back here." I reorganized the entire backroom during my earlier shift, dividing titles by genre. Her romance and fantasy shelves are the most bare, simply because those are the titles she seems to sell the most of. "Luckily, these are all signed. You move these fast, don't you?"

"It depends on which book it is." She peeks into the boxes, a look of relief washing over her. "But yes, these will move quickly. We can even put some out on the floor because I sold out of this one in a day." She points to the market's current most popular book. "I don't know how many more I'll receive of them signed."

I try to maintain a look of disinterest when I ask, "How did you manage to get them signed in the first place?"

She bends over to try and lift a box of hardcovers, then

blows her bangs off her forehead with a resigned sigh. I decide to spare her the humiliation of having to ask for my help—just this once—and lift the box with ease, following her to a table at the front of the store.

"I have a lot of great relationships with agents. Before I opened, I tried to build connections with publishers. It didn't go badly, but nothing was sticking. It wasn't until I started attending book conventions in large cities that I made headway. Agents loved the idea of their author's books being in indie bookstores."

I listen intently while assisting with unpacking the books. "But don't box stores move larger amounts of inventory quicker?"

"Sure," she says with a shrug. "But ever since the pandemic, reading has become more about bonding with like-minded individuals. It's a community more than it's ever been. Much of my customer base is made of friend groups who want to come in just to bond over their love for reading. They come in, they grab some coffee, and they just…. Talk. To me, to each other. And then we exchange socials and keep the conversation going digitally."

My brow furrows. "And authors want this?"

She breaks down the empty box, sticking the pieces of tape to her jeans. "Most authors I've met want to connect with their readers. Authors write the stories, but readers *share* the stories. You might have more options when you walk into a box store, but you're missing intimacy. When you walk into my store, I want you to feel like you're friends with me. I'll push an author's book until I'm blue in the face. Do you get that from your typical box store? Sure, there are exceptions, but turnover rates are so fast that it makes it difficult to establish relationships."

I think back to the moment during my first visit to Shoreline Scribes and how protective the customer seemed over Fallon and her table of annotated books. Her customers think of her as their friend, which builds trust and keeps them returning. FFJ's stores might have some employees who think like Fallon, but they don't have the time to stop and have in-depth conversations with each customer.

Fallon prioritizes it.

Fallon's phone pings with a text notification, and she pauses to pull her phone from her jeans. With an eye roll, she reads the text and drops her phone to the table.

I ask, "Everything okay?"

She waves her hand dismissively. "The impromptu delivery is courtesy of this author's agent. He wants a little more with me than the standard agent-and-book-store-owner relationship. He's in town and wants to grab dinner later."

My hand flexes at my side. "Oh? Are you going?"

She glances down at her clothing, pulling the tape from her jeans and smoothing it over the cardboard box. "I don't have time to change, but it's an important relationship I need to maintain. I'll have him meet me somewhere close to my apartment. Hopefully, it won't last too long."

Close to her apartment? So he can come over after?

I need to ensure that won't happen.

*fallon*

I was correct in assuming I'd have no time before meeting Ryan for dinner. I didn't know he was coming to town, but the extra shipments of books from his author should've tipped me off. I don't think he would expect dinner with me in exchange for books, but I also don't want to risk the relationship. The newest book release is the first in a series. I'd love to continue receiving signed copies for the next installment, so I must maintain my friendship with Ryan. He's pulled back on sending me self-ies, so maybe he's accepted that a friendship is *all* I want from him.

Ryan is already seated in the restaurant that is far too fancy for what I'm wearing. Thank God they don't have a dress code because that's precisely the embarrassment I would never recover from. But fuck, a steak sounds divine.

"Fallon!"

I hear him calling my name over the soft music playing from overhead speakers, though he doesn't need to shout at all. I already spotted him when I walked in. He is dressed for a place like this, but he doesn't say anything about what I'm wearing when he stands to greet me.

I do.

"I didn't have time to change after I received your text." I try to smooth my hair down. I had a brush in my bag, at least. Getting the knots out of my Rapunzel-esque hair was a bitch.

"You look fantastic, Fallon." He kisses my temple during our side hug.

That's a little more intimate than usual.

I clear my throat while sitting in the chair positioned across from him. "Thank you. And thank you for the books. The first shipment sold out immediately, so I appreciate you securing more for me."

He places his hand over mine and squeezes. "Of course."

He's never touched me this much in such a short time. I have a feeling he's expecting a little more than dinner tonight. And don't get me wrong—Ryan is a catch. Sleeping with him wouldn't be horrible. But doing it in exchange for books seems… transactional and *icky*.

And I don't have feelings for him. Sex has never been a hobby for me. I've read too many books. Romanticized it too much. I envy people who can sleep with someone simply for pleasure. Unfortunately, my attachment style attaches a little too hard to men with whom I share intimate moments.

I blow out a slow breath and peruse the menu. Since sitting down, my stomach has twisted into knots, and a steak doesn't sound as appetizing as when I walked in. "It was such a long day," I say, focusing on the lighter portion of the menu. "We trained a new employee, and the extra shipments have worn me out. I might not be able to stay out late tonight."

Ryan doesn't mask his disappointment when he frowns. The need to please people gnaws at me, but I can't cross that boundary with him. Too much is at risk if it were to go south between us. Plus… well, Fitz shouldn't be a reason at all.

Yet, he is. He was helpful today. My initial judgment of him might've been wrong. I mean, yes, he's arrogant. But he's also intelligent and inquisitive. Beautiful. Mysterious. And I find myself thinking of him outside of the store.

"How long are you in town for?" I inquire, breaking the silence. I can squeeze a coffee date into my schedule if he's not leaving tomorrow. Aside from the books, I genuinely enjoy Ryan's company. He travels often and always has a story to tell me. "I'll be at the book convention in Los Angeles again. That's in a couple weeks, right?"

"I leave the day after tomorrow. The convention in Los Angeles is sold out." He pauses while the server leaves us glasses of wine. He must've ordered these before I arrived. "There's supposed to be a thousand people there. It'll be a great time for you to build more connections."

"Oh!" I smack my forehead. "I have the business cards for the goody bags. Thank you again for including them."

Finally, he smiles again. "Of course. Alyssa will include them in the bag with the event exclusive special edition."

I lean forward and whisper, "Can I snag one of those?"

He matches my energy, leaning toward me to reply, "I have one in my suitcase with your name on it."

I clap my hands together excitedly. "You're the absolute best, Ryan. Not that I need another edition. I can't wait until the second book releases. How is Alyssa handling the sudden attention? I imagine it's a lot of pressure."

His earlier joy morphs into a sigh as he slumps back in his chair. "She's overwhelmed. She went from having time to write whenever she pleases to interviews and meetings while still having a deadline for the next book."

I take a sip of my wine. "If Alyssa ever needs a break, she can come and write in my living room. I'm hardly home anyway. It could be a little oasis for her."

Grabbing my hand, Ryan kisses one of my knuckles. "I will offer that to her, Fallon. You're always so generous."

I'm about to pull my hand away when a familiar scent wafts over me. It hits me all at once, and I turn my head, searching. I spot him at the bar two tables away from us. His back is to me, but his head is turned, giving me a glimpse of his steep jawline. Fitz. Fitz is *here*.

"Um," I fumble, taking my hand back. What do I do? Do I stand up and greet him? Call him over? Would Ryan consider that rude? We haven't ordered yet. Maybe Fitz wants to do more than sit at the bar and drink. I didn't tell him I was coming here, did I? If I had, I doubt he would've come.

"Fitz!" I didn't fully finish processing my thoughts before his name came tumbling from my lips.

Ryan follows my gaze just as Fitz looks over his shoulder at me. He hasn't changed since he left the store, either. Maybe he was craving a steak, too. It is what this restaurant is known for.

I wave. Why the fuck did I just wave?

Beer in hand, Fitz stands from the barstool and coolly saunters toward us. Ryan looks from me to Fitz again, but I can't stop studying Fitz. *What is he doing here?* Of all the restaurants in Sanderling, did he happen to stumble into the one where I'm having dinner? "Fitz," I say, warmer than anticipated. It's not like I just saw this man an hour ago. "Have you eaten?"

Fitz takes that as an invitation to sit in the empty chair between Ryan and me, sliding a menu from the table and popping it open. "I haven't. I heard this place has the best steaks in all of New Hampshire." Then, he glances at Ryan and extends his hand. "Fitz. I work with Fallon."

"Th-this is your new employee?" Ryan asks, blinking.

I take a long sip from my wine glass. "In the flesh. Fitz,

this is Ryan. He's Alyssa's agent, which is why we received more signed copies of her book today."

"Ah," Fitz replies, perusing the menu. He seems about as interested in my company as he would be watching paint dry. "We had a long evening of unpacking those together." Fitz glances up with a slight grin. "Thanks."

I don't stop drinking from my glass until the wine is gone, and Fitz signals for more, watching me with a hint of amusement. "Thirsty, Fallon?" he asks with a smug smirk.

Ryan rolls his shoulders back. "Fallon will be visiting me in a couple weeks. She attends a book convention in Los Angeles every year. It's actually how we met—"

"Interesting," Fitz interrupts, placing the menu on the table and resting his elbow on the table, leaning slightly closer to me while maintaining eye contact with Ryan. "She mentioned conventions earlier. It would be a great learning opportunity for me if I attended one with her."

My gaze bounces back and forth between Fitz and Ryan like a game of Ping Pong. Are they… fighting over me? This would probably be a moment of swooning if I were a main character in a romance novel, but right now, it just feels too hot, and I might start sweating soon.

*Change the subject.*

"Fitz." I pull his gaze back to me. "I know you're from Boston, but I never asked what brought you to Sanderling."

Fitz finishes the content of his bottle, his eyes pinned to mine like we're the only ones in the restaurant. And for a delusional moment, I think his reason for moving here is me, though that would be impossible. But I don't mind imagining being the reason why someone like him abandoned his home. The constant mystery surrounding him is one of his biggest draws—that *and* his love for classics.

Fitz lowers his bottle to the table. "I needed a change of scenery. I've been in Boston my entire life. I've visited

New Hampshire many times, but Sanderling has always interested me. I didn't want to be only a tourist anymore."

His reasoning for coming here is similar to mine. I needed to be away from home. I needed to be somewhere completely different, where familiar scenery wouldn't trigger memories.

"And you just stumbled into Fallon's store?" Ryan asks, and I'd forgotten he was here for a moment.

Fitz slowly nods but never looks away from me. "I had read about her store in our local paper. It was highlighting small businesses in New Hampshire."

I have a copy of the paper he's referring to. Thomas was so excited when his friend told him about the insert that he nearly knocked over a shelf of books when he ran into the store, waving the paper around like a lunatic. He'd driven to Boston early that morning to snag a copy for us. I don't have it hanging up at the store like the article about Shoreline Scribes being the business to watch, but it does have a nice, permanent location on my desk. Maybe my dreams of expanding into Boston will someday be realized.

# *hayes*

I didn't plan to invite myself to sit and eat dinner with Fallon and Ryan, but after seeing him kiss her hand earlier, I couldn't resist the urge to plant myself between them. Fallon didn't look interested in him, anyway. I might've been doing her a favor. She seemed only a little suspicious about how I ended up at the same restaurant as her, but she never brought it up.

And now, I need to complete the evening by offering to take her home before Ryan does. I've deduced that Fallon doesn't have a car. She either rides with Thomas, takes public transport, or walks everywhere, which is typical in a city as small as Sanderling. As cold as it is outside, I wish she had something for the winter months.

I watch as she pulls her hair out from the collar of her puffer jacket, and my mind wanders to what it'd be like to gather it in my fist. It's long enough to twist around my wrist. "I'll take you home," I tell her before Ryan can offer the same.

This time, she doesn't try to argue with me. Ryan looks at me like I just bought the last piece of his favorite candy, but he quickly hides it when Fallon goes in for a goodbye hug. He wraps his arms around her tighter than he should, and I don't believe it's purely to piss me off. He wants her. I could tell the second I saw them together. She's a challenge for him. I recognized the look in his eyes as the same one Jace gets when he wants to conquer someone.

I know his type. He's used to getting the women he wants. It's evident by his socials. When Fallon mentioned having relationships with agents, I looked into who Alyssa's is and discovered Ryan. His feed contains pictures of himself and what it's like living in Los Angeles—more of the former. I found Fallon because he primarily follows women and a few gym rats. Her profile isn't private—it can't be based on how personable she is—but her feed is bare. A few aesthetic shots of her tennis shoes or a water bottle atop a yoga mat, some of her store, but nothing truly personal.

Ryan has liked all her pictures.

Surprisingly, I didn't find an account for Shoreline Scribes, meaning her popularity has been purely through word of mouth. I can't imagine how much more it'd blow up if she promoted through static posts, but time isn't on her side. She's already taken on so much, even with Thomas' help.

When she pries herself away from Ryan, I hold my elbow out for her to grab. To my surprise, she does. She slides her hand through the crook of my arm like it's second nature. "Are you in a rush to get home?" I ask, peering down at her. It's late. We're both exhausted. But there's a place I want to visit, and I want her to experience it with me.

I see her mind working in the way her eyes search the parking lot. She isn't looking for my car. She's shuffling through the multiple papers in her mind. I want to urge her to relax, but I learned quickly that Fallon cannot be pushed. She has a gentle exterior, but she's scrappy internally. Until me, it seems Fallon kept her circle close and controlled. Predictable.

I want to bleed through her edges.

Finally, she stops thinking of why she shouldn't come with me and slightly shakes her head. "Not in a rush."

Wordlessly, I lead her through the parking lot, not to the rental car from the other night but to my bike. It was dropped off right before dinner. And the sudden hesitancy in her walk causes me to chuckle, continuing to pull her alongside me. "It's safer than you think," I assure her. "I've been riding for years and haven't wrecked. Skidded, maybe."

"Lovely," she mutters under her breath.

With a grin, I produce gloves for her to slide on. "Trust me, you'll be glad for those when the wind hits." After she slides them on, I take the passenger helmet and gently slide it over her head. Her smushed cheeks widen my grin, and I tighten the chinstrap without a word.

She rolls her eyes, acutely aware of how she must look. "Are you jealous I look better than you in a helmet?" she asks in jest, but she is completely correct. She's adorable.

Pulling my phone from my jacket pocket, I raise it and snap a picture before she can protest. "Blackmail," I say.

She smacks my stomach with a gasp, and I slam her visor shut. It slips from her grasp when she tries to pry it open, primarily thanks to the leather gloves but also because she's never worn one. "I should fire you," she shouts since her voice is muffled beneath the helmet.

"You should," I confirm before sliding my helmet on and straddling the seat. "Throw your leg over, Fallon."

She mounts the bike with ease, and I have to turn my head to stare straight ahead. Adjusting her body to fit tightly against mine, I stiffen when her arms slide around my waist. She's either afraid, or this isn't the first bike she's been on. "You're a pro," I shout, curiosity winning over.

I feel her rest her head against my back. "I didn't realize it was rocket science," she retorts.

"Okay, smartass." I jolt us, laughing when she squeals and tightens her hold on me. "Cling much?" Her fingers dig into my ribcage, and I flick her hand away. "This isn't great passenger etiquette, you know?"

The laughter in her voice when she asks, "Do you know how to drive this, or do you just talk shit?" keeps me smiling the entire ride.

---

The wind bites against my skin as I pull my motorcycle to a stop in front of the old lighthouse. It's been out of service for years, but something about it has always called to me. Maybe it's the isolation or the way the waves crash against the rocks below, creating a steady rhythm that drowns out all the noise in my head.

I remove my helmet and turn to Fallon, who's been silent most of the ride. Her eyes are fixed on the lighthouse as she removes her helmet, and I see the same awe in her that I feel each time I see it. "I've never been here," she whispers, her voice soft, like she's sharing a secret with me.

I smile, trying to push away the tension that's been building between us. "I thought you'd like it. It's peaceful out here. No distractions."

Her footsteps are light against the gravel, and her body language is guarded. She's curious but cautious, which happens to be how I feel each time I'm near her.

We climb the worn steps of the lighthouse, the wind howling around us. When we reach the top, I step aside to let her take in the view. She looks out at the dark horizon, her back to me, and I see her shoulders relax just a little bit as the weight of the world seems to melt away.

"Wow," she murmurs, her voice awestruck. "I didn't think it'd be this beautiful up here. I never imagined it."

I stand behind her, close enough for her to feel my presence but far enough to keep a distance between us. "I don't believe that for a second."

Her wild hair flows freely down her back when she shakes her head in disagreement. "I moved here and immediately started working. I know surprisingly little about Sanderling."

This is my chance to learn a little more about her. "And where did you come from, Fallon Madison?"

In an instant, her shoulders turn inward, and her chin drops slightly. I've hit a nerve. Maybe the question should've been, *what are you running away from?*

I step closer, inches spared between us. "You're such a little tragedy with all your secrets, aren't you?"

She spins when she hears the soft condescension in my voice. Her eyes flare when she notices the lack of space between our bodies, but she doesn't step away. Instead, she squares her shoulders. "And what about you, *Fitz*? Don't think I didn't peek at your paperwork today."

I shrug a shoulder. "You have my social security number and last name. You don't need my entire name. I never go by my first name. At least you know where I'm from."

She releases a slow breath. "Missouri."

I already knew that, of course. The name of her university was on her sweatshirt the day we met. "Missouri," I repeat. "And what is a business major from Missouri doing in New Hampshire? It's quite different than what you're used to."

She raises an eyebrow. "How did you know I was a business major?"

This time, it's my turn to roll my eyes. "You have one

of the best new businesses in the state, Fallon. It's not hard to correctly assume what you studied."

"I just..." she trails off and turns away. "I love the water."

The water she *just* admitted to never imagining? That's a bullshit reason, and we both know it. I'm not going to push her for more right now. She could fire me on the spot, and this entire idea of mine would have been for nothing.

I watch her momentarily, the way the moonlight catches in her hair and her hands grip the railing. There's something about this place that makes everything feel... different. Time moves slower here, and the past and future don't matter. Only the present.

"I come to Sanderling to think," I admit, leaning against the wall next to her. "When I need to escape every-thing. My father, work... everything. It's the only place I've found where I don't feel I must be someone else."

That was more honest than anticipated.

Fallon faces me again, her eyes searching mine for some-thing. "And what do you think about when you come here?"

I don't answer right away. Instead, I let the question hang in the air, its weight almost suffocating. I've always avoided discussing my family, my father's expectations, and how he controls every part of my life. But with Fallon, something feels different. Maybe I don't have to lie to her about everything. I can let her in a little.

"I think about what it would be like to live without him," I finally say, my voice rougher than I intended. "To just... walk away from all of it. But then I think about the price. The sacrifices. And I'm unsure if I'm strong enough to make those choices."

Fallon is silent for a long time, her gaze floating between me and the view. She seems to be weighing my words against something inside her.

"You don't have to do everything he says," she says finally, her voice gentle. "You can choose for yourself. You just have to be willing to risk everything for it."

Her words struck me harder than I expected, leaving me unsure what to say. It can't ever be that simple. I can't walk away from everything I've known.

I shake my head, confusion and anger bubbling up inside me. "I don't have the luxury of just... choosing. There are consequences. People's lives are tied to his business. My father built something, and I—" Careful, Fitz. Rein it back.

"You don't have to carry all that on your own," she interrupts, facing me fully now. Her eyes are soft and understanding, but their intensity makes me feel seen in a way I haven't been in years. "Believe me, Fitz. Life is too short."

This is too much too soon. I wasn't expecting a deep conversation with her tonight, even though I was the one to initiate it. But the pressure in my chest causes me to close off again.

I tuck a strand of hair behind her ear, avoiding the weight of the moment between us. "It's been a long day. Let's get you home."

*fallon*

With Thomas unable to come into the store today, I hoped it'd be a slow day, but the universe played its wily tricks and increased our foot traffic. It's the first day in a while that the sun is shining brightly on Sanderling, giving its residents a taste of the upcoming spring. I had to pull Fitz from the back and train him to ring up customers. It's been entertaining watching him interact with the gawking women. They either bluntly flirt with him or stutter their way through the transaction. Fitz treats each one the same, though.

With disinterest. He isn't rude, just… distant.

I hate to admit that I dressed a little cuter today. With a short black skirt over brown tights, a maroon turtleneck, and black boots, I fit the aesthetic of a quirky bookstore owner well—at least according to Pinterest, which I used when trying to put together an outfit from my outdated closet. I should find more time to do things outside of Pilates.

Fitz is more casual than usual today. He picked up on the fact that he would always leave this store with scuff marks somewhere on his body. He's covered in black from head to toe. Black Dr. Martens, black jeans, black tee. The only color on him is the blue of his eyes. I can tell he tried to gel his hair to keep it out of his eyes, but the constant shuffling around the store has made a few strands fall handsomely over his forehead. Who am I trying to kid?

The man is visually pleasing.

I tried to find him on socials when he dropped me off at home last night, but I came up empty-handed with only 'Fitz' to really go off. I can't help but be curious about the little he shared last night. From what I could gather, he is trying to avoid working for his father. I wanted to ask more questions, but he cut the conversation short.

Sore subject, I suppose.

When he finishes bagging books for a young girl, he glances my way and grins when he catches me staring at him. I duck my head and squeeze my eyes shut, falling forward to slump against the bookshelf. I'm supposed to be shelving, but I can't stop looking at him. He's picked up on the business so effortlessly. I'd be lying if I said I wasn't a little impressed. When I first met him, he didn't seem like the type to have ever worked a day in his life.

"Has Fitz worn you down?"

I nearly drop the books in my arms. When I glance up, it takes me a few seconds to recognize the man beside me. "Jace," I say when his name registers. "No, not at all." I shuffle the books into one arm and motion toward Fitz at the register. "He's right there if you're looking for him."

Jace leans his shoulder against the bookshelf, crossing his arms loosely over his chest. "I'm content where I am."

"Right… okay." I busy myself with searching for where to place one of this year's most popular books. We had a table full of them earlier this year, but the hype has died down enough to put them on a shelf. "What brings you in?"

Jace checks the time on his watch. "Almost closing time,

right? I'm here to convince Fitz to join me for a night at an exclusive jazz lounge in Sanderling. Have you been?"

I wrinkle my nose. "I didn't realize we had those here."

"There's a few scattered between here and Boston." Jace takes the books from my arms and follows me to the next shelf. "You just haven't been hanging out with the right people. Don't worry; I'll get you in this evening."

I put away a book from his stack. "Oh, I don't know if I'm dressed for a jazz club, and I don't have anything at home—"

"Nonsense," he interrupts. "You look great. And if Fitz turns me down, at least I'll have you."

I part my lips to decline his offer but pause when Fitz appears behind Jace, his head cocked slightly. "Turn you down for what, Jace?"

With a cocky grin, Jace turns and shoves the books into Fitz's chest. "We're going to a jazz lounge this evening, Fitz. You're more than welcome to join us."

I want to argue that there isn't an *us*—that I was about to deny the offer altogether, but Fitz doesn't need my reassurance. All it takes is a look shared between us to gather that information on his own. "We had dinner plans, but if Fallon is okay with changing them, we'll join you."

I'm not aware of any plans, but I play along. "As appetizing as sub sandwiches sound, I'd be okay experiencing a jazz lounge tonight instead."

Jace clicks his tongue. "Damn, Fitz. Sub sandwiches. You're really pulling out all the stops, aren't you?"

I shove my tongue into my cheek to try and stop a smile from forming. I suppose I could've said something… classier, but sub sandwiches sound delicious. I planned to make one when I got home tonight, but it sounds like I'll eat my words at a jazz lounge instead.

The low hum of conversation fills the air as we descend the stairs into the exclusive underground jazz lounge. The dim lighting and the soft glow of chandeliers create an intimate, almost secretive atmosphere. The sound of a saxophone pours over the room, smooth and soulful, winding its way around our table like a seductive whisper.

I glance at Fitz, who has been unusually quiet since we arrived. His expression is unreadable, but I can feel the weight of his gaze on me. Next to him, Jace is in his usual cocky, relaxed element, scanning the crowd and smirking at anyone who dares to make eye contact.

"This place is a hidden gem," Jace says with a grin, leaning back in his chair as he watches a couple take the floor to dance. "Wouldn't expect you to be into jazz, Fallon. Thought you'd be more of a pop music kind of girl."

I raise an eyebrow, picking up the wine freshly delivered to our table. "I have a wide range of tastes, Jace. I'm full of surprises."

Jace chuckles, clearly intrigued but not intimidated. "I bet you are."

I shift uncomfortably, noticing the tension between him and Fitz. It isn't just because of me; I know that, but I can't help feeling caught in the middle of their quiet competition. Fitz, ever the enigma, seems distant and focused on the stage, but I can sense something stirring beneath his calm exterior.

On the other hand, Jace is playing the part of the charming bad boy, always teasing and flirting. It would make sense that they'd both be attracted to me, but I can't shake the feeling that Jace sees it as more of a game than anything else. He and Fitz are close; that much is obvious, but something is lurking beneath the surface of their friendship.

As the music swells, Fitz leans in, breaking the silence.

"You're not planning to stay seated all night, right?" His voice is low, a hint of amusement threading through the words.

"Why?" I tease. "You think I can't handle a little dancing?"

Fitz's lips quirk up into the smallest of smiles, a hint of something deeper flickering in his eyes. "I don't think you can, Fallon. I *know* you can." He stands and offers me his hand.

The first song is slow, seductive, and full of emotion. Fitz leads, his hand firm on my waist as we sway together. His body is close to mine, and his movements are smooth and confident. There's something magnetic about how he moves—like he isn't just dancing with me but genuinely connecting with me. My heart races from the palpable tension between us.

"You're a good dancer," I murmur, my voice barely a whisper above the music.

Fitz smiles, but there's a softness in his eyes that I haven't noticed before. "You make it easy."

As we dance, I glimpse Jace out of the corner of my eye. He's watching us, his posture casual, but I can see the slight clenching of his jaw. There's something about him that screams competition, even though he tries to play it off as if it's nothing.

"You and Jace," I begin, refocusing on Fitz. "How long have you been friends?"

"Since childhood," he replies dryly, his hold on my waist tightening slightly. "He's my best friend... well, one of them."

"Andrew is the other," I assume aloud. "I feel like a chess piece between the two of you."

Fitz slows and places his index finger beneath my chin, ensuring he holds my gaze. "Only if you're something to be won, Fallon. Otherwise, you don't need to play the game."

My pulse is thundering, and I wonder for a moment if he can hear it over the music. "I'm not interested in playing."

"No?" Fitz suddenly spins me out and back in, and I catch myself by placing my palms against his chest. "Then what's your story, Fallon? Why are you in New Hampshire?"

"I told you," I snap. "I wanted something different. I like being near the water. Why are you so interested in me?"

"Because you're not being truthful." His hands find my waist. We're no longer keeping in rhythm with the beat of the music, but he doesn't seem to care. "I recognize secrets when I see them, and you've got one."

I'm unable to hold his gaze because he's right. I left Missouri for a specific reason, but he hasn't earned the right to know why yet. And certainly not here, when his friend stares at me like I'm a piece of meat to be devoured. But Fitz… he looks at me differently. Still something to be consumed, but it's deeper than that. More like he wants to savor me instead.

Finally, I tilt my chin up and lock eyes with him. "You know what they say, Fitz. Curiosity killed the cat."

He lowers me into a dip and follows, leaning in close enough to feel the warmth of his breath against my throat. "I'm willing to risk it to satisfy my interest, Fallon."

When the song ends, Fitz silently leads me back to the table, his hand still resting on the small of my back. But as soon as I sit down, Jace stands up, offering me his hand with a grin that's all cockiness. "It's my turn."

The second song is faster and more playful. Jace doesn't hold back, pulling me into the rhythm with him.

He moves with that same confident swagger, his grin wide as he spins me around the dance floor.

"You're not like the others," Jace murmurs, his voice low as we twirl. "You know that, right?"

I raise an eyebrow, not sure where this conversation is headed. "What do you mean?"

He grins again, but it's no longer lighthearted. It's sharper, like a challenge. "You're different. That's why he likes you. But you should move cautiously, Fallon. Fitz has a reputation."

I take my earlier advice and don't try to dissect what Jace is saying. I could ask more questions, but I won't like any of the answers he gives me. I'd rather remain naive about the man who walked into my store only a few days ago and has done nothing but cause mayhem and chaos in my life. He's uprooted my carefully planned days and consistent, sometimes dull schedule. He's trying to force himself into places I've long boarded up. And it's working.

He's getting under my skin.

I catch Fitz's gaze across the room. He's watching us, his arms crossed, a slight scowl pulling at his lips. It's subtle, but it's there. And suddenly, the air between Jace and me shifts. The tension between the three of us simmers, unspoken and raw. I feel the pull between Fitz and Jace, a quiet war being waged over me, and I don't know how to handle it.

The longer I stay wedged between them, the harder it becomes to keep my emotions in check. I need to get out of here to breathe and think. "I'm stepping outside for a bit," I announce, parting from Jace and beelining for the way out.

# *hayes*

When Fallon rushes out, I stand. My patience wears thin as Jace casually strolls back to our table and takes a sip from his glass. He ordered a house drink full of vermouth. "What the fuck did you say to her, Jace?"

Jace swirls the drink around in his glass with a casual shrug. "I just warned her, Fitz. I said you love a challenge."

I could kill him where he stands, but that would really wrench my plans. "You realize you could fuck this entire thing up for me, right? My father is relying on me to learn as much about her as possible."

He sits and curls his arm around the back of Fallon's empty chair. He's acting like he doesn't care, but I know him better than that. He's allowing this years-long competition between us to affect something that could make a difference in my relationship with my father. "What do you want?" I'm willing to make it happen for him to keep quiet about this. "Do you want a position in the company?"

He finishes his drink and signals the server for another. He's not rushing to reply because he knows I'm waiting to chase after Fallon. "No, Fitz. I don't give a fuck about working for your father. What I want is a little steeper than that."

My mind immediately goes into overdrive, causing every nerve ending to stand on edge. Jace has always lusted after everything I have, but the only thing he doesn't have so far is…

"Fallon," he finishes. "You're betting a lot on her, which means she must be worth more than a simple rundown of her store. You want to break her." He stands and rests his hands on the back of his chair. "You think I don't know you? I do. All the twisted games you play with the women in your life? Fallon isn't like them, and you want to find out what makes her tick. I just want to be the one to pick up the pieces when you succeed in tearing her apart."

My nostrils flare as I try to keep my temper in check. "Is that why you fucked Raquel, Jace? You can't find a woman alone, so you are waiting for my discards?" I didn't want to give Jace the satisfaction of knowing he hit a nerve when I learned about him and Raquel, but what he's asking for is lower than anything I've had to put up with from him over the years.

He circles the table and grabs my shoulder, squeezing. I clench my fists. The last thing I need is to be escorted out of the lounge and have Fallon witness it if she's still outside, but punching Jace almost seems worth it. "Just think of me as your cleanup crew, Fitz. Do we have a deal?"

I don't care what it takes—Jace will never touch her. But I nod once to satisfy him and buy myself more time to see this plan through. "Yeah, asshole. Deal."

I carry Fallon's jacket outside. She left it on her chair in her rush to get away from Jace, and I doubt she'd get far without it before eventually circling back. She's stubborn, but she's not stupid. And that's precisely what she's doing when I find her. She's practically stomping down the sidewalk, muttering something under her breath and twisting her hair through her fingers. He activated her anxiety, the returning tension evident in her shoulders.

"Looking for this?" I ask, holding her jacket out.

Her lips clamp shut as she looks up, but she doesn't lunge quickly enough before I hold it up and out of her reach. "Come back inside, Fallon."

"No," she says through clenched teeth.

Since I'm not cruel, I put her jacket on her, even going as far as to zip it up to keep her from bolting. "Fine, we won't go back in. I'll take you home."

She plants her finger against my chest. "I don't want you to take me home. I can get there on my own."

She only had one glass of wine, but I can tell she's bordering on tipsy, and her frustration will only add to her delirium. She's also exhausted. We've worked hard these last two days. I shouldn't have brought her tonight, especially given the kind of mood Jace was in.

I grab her jacket pocket when she tries to turn away from me, tugging her back. "It's freezing, Fallon. I'm not letting you walk home from here. Do you even know where we are?"

She folds her arms over her chest, defiant in how she holds her chin. "I've lived here for over a year. I think I can recognize street signs, Fitz."

I release her. "Okay. Which direction is your apartment?"

She spins back and forth on her heels, gnawing on her bottom lip. Sure, maybe during the day, she could recognize where she is, but after a drink, I have my doubts at night. Fallon is hardheaded but also cold, so I'm curious to see how long she'll hold out before she admits defeat.

I don't know if it's a nervous habit, but she starts braiding her hair, producing a band from her wrist to secure the end. "Fine," she says after a couple minutes pass. "You can take me home, but only because I'm freezing."

I hold out my arm for her to grab. "Understood."

When we arrive at her building, Fallon bypasses the entrance to her apartment and instead wanders into the small grocery store connected to it. I'm unsure why I follow her inside, but I want to make sure she makes it twenty feet back to her apartment before I leave her for the evening.

It would make sense that she's hungry. We left the lounge before our food was delivered to the table. I texted Jace before we left, letting him know that Fallon was tired and wanted to go home. He hasn't responded, and I have no doubt that it's because he's annoyed he couldn't further his agenda with her by flirting some more. Just the thought of him being near her sends me into a tailspin. He's only interested in her because I've gotten close, and Jace always needs to prove to himself that he can have whatever I have.

But he won't get Fallon.

As she walks down an aisle, she glances over her shoulder, unsurprised by me following her. In fact, she smiles and turns to walk backward. Her tired eyes are glazed, but she exudes energy I haven't seen yet. "Are you hungry, Fitz?"

Fuck, I am. But not strictly for food.

In two steps, I'm close enough to her to spin the end of her braid around my finger. "Starved. Do you know what sounds good, Fallon?"

She licks her lips, her gaze dropping to mine only briefly. "Tell me," she murmurs.

I lean in closer and step into her so she has to back up a small step, her hands fisting my shirt instinctively. I did that on purpose, of course. The fear of falling backward is guaranteed to get someone to latch onto you. We're practically glued together in the middle of the spice aisle. Anyone walking past could mistake this moment as the one when I'm about to kiss her. But I know she wants it, so I must wait a little longer.

Instead, I tug slightly on her braid and whisper, "Sub sandwiches and chips. And beer."

She throws her head back in the sweetest laugh, using her hold on my shirt to drag me down a different aisle. "Luckily for you, I'm a pro at making sandwiches."

---

The inside of Fallon's apartment is just how I imagined it'd be. Like the bookstore, it's cozy. She has blankets and throws tossed over her couch and in a basket in the corner of her living room; her fireplace is decorated with books and trinkets that look like they came from thrift stores, and a table for two sits in the small nook connected to her kitchen. From already looking at her floor plan online, I know she only has one bedroom, which sits behind the living room, unlit.

She lights a vanilla-scented candle on her kitchen counter before removing the ingredients we chose from the bags I carried up. "Make yourself at home," she says, gesturing toward her living room.

"There's that southern charm," I say, moving behind her to take two beers from the case instead.

She snorts, slicing the bread. "Missouri is considered a midwestern state, although some places, mostly those closest to Arkansas, might identify more southern, I guess."

Good. She's talking about it. "And which part of Missouri are you from? What do you identify as?"

I think it helps that she's distracted with making the sandwiches. It doesn't give her time to hesitate. "I haven't given it much thought," she replies, spreading mayonnaise. "I ramble like a midwesterner. I'll talk to anyone about anything."

I craft my questions carefully. "Did you go to school close to home?"

She nods while arranging tomato slices. "I lived in the same town as Mizzou. Tuition was cheaper for in-state students, so I lived at home while attending."

That means she hasn't been on her own for long. After putting the bottles on the counter next to her, I step behind her and slowly remove her jacket, causing her to stop what she's doing to allow it. The tension between us is suffocating, especially when she leans just enough for the back of her head to brush against my chest. "Thank you," she whispers.

It takes considerable effort to step away from her, but I walk to the other side of the counter to drape her jacket over a barstool, then add mine atop hers. "I've traveled a lot, but never to Missouri. Do you go home often?"

And then that look returns, where she disassociates and distances herself. "The store has done so well that I don't have time for much else. I'm almost finished."

My brow furrows. What did she leave behind that left her so shattered that she can't talk about it? Did she have her heart broken? Did she leave a man behind? I don't see any framed pictures around her apartment. Was there a falling out with her parents? I felt no tension when she brought up the story about her mom. It was one of the few times she seemed relaxed around me.

I decide not to push her any more about it tonight. Instead, I return to her side and assist in plating the sandwiches and chips we chose, following her to the table. "Thank you for feeding me tonight," I say, sitting across from her. "I apologize for Jace."

She studies me while taking her first bite, waiting until she takes a sip of beer before she asks, "Why do you stay friends with him?"

I grin, purely because I've asked myself that question multiple times. "There's a lot of history, and despite our recent history, Jace has been there during many difficult times. He was with me when I discovered one of my father's affairs. We walked into the office and caught them in the act."

Her eyes widen. "Fitz, I'm so sorry."

I pop a chip into my mouth and shrug. "It is what it is. But he took me to get drunk afterward and never spoke of it again. Jace knows how to be a great friend. He just allows his ego to get the best of him sometimes."

When Fallon's cell phone rings, she rolls her eyes and stands, dusting her hands off. "That's my ringtone for Thomas. Even though he has my location, he checks in every night. I think he's afraid I'll croak someday and be alone."

Leaning back in the chair, I watch her move through the kitchen. "Well, you're not alone tonight. I promise to report any dead bodies to him."

*hayes*

Moments pass as she speaks with Thomas, leaving out the dramatic details of our night but informing him where she's been and how I'm sitting at her table, eating a carefully crafted sandwich. She doesn't mention that I'm staring at her or that she keeps looking at me with a flirty smile, unable to control the red blossoming on her cheeks.

And I don't know what it is about this particular moment—if it's watching her in her natural environment, disarmed and charming, or if it's because she's talking to another man, even though I know it's purely platonic—but I stand and slowly walk toward her. She pulls her bottom lip between her teeth as she watches me, humming bland replies to whatever Thomas says on the other side of the line.

Wordlessly, I dip and grab the back of her thighs, hoisting her up and onto the counter. Her little gasp in response makes me grin, but I shake my head when she opens her mouth to undoubtedly end her phone call. "Don't hang up," I demand.

She's still in her short skirt and tights, and the partial gap between her legs has me salivating for what's waiting, but I want to play with her a little first.

She stutters her way through the call, tracking my movements intensely as I grab a fresh beer from the pack and twist the lid off. I take a couple sips first, the corner of my mouth tilted up in a sinister grin. She's anticipating my next move, aching for me to touch her again. It's how she's been since this morning when she couldn't stop watching me work. She studied every interaction I had with a woman, not realizing I noticed all of it.

I return to stand in front of her, pushing her knees apart so I can stand between her legs. Her skirt stretches tightly around her thighs. "Did you tell Thomas about the books Ryan sent to you?" I take another swig of beer. "Did you tell him about your dinner?"

"The dinner you crashed?" she asks in reply, raising her eyebrow in challenge. "No, I haven't."

"Do it." Grabbing her chin, I push her head back a couple inches. "But open your mouth first."

Her eyes search mine, but then she parts her lips. Using my hold on her chin, I pry her mouth open a little more. "So responsive," I murmur, dragging my thumb across her bottom lip while taking a drink from my bottle.

Then, I lean in and spit the beer into her mouth.

I hear Thomas ask if she's okay when she coughs a little from surprise, drops of beer spilling from the corner of her mouth. I use my index finger to scoop them up, sliding my finger between her lips to return it. Instinctively, she closes her lips around my finger and sucks, sending a jolt straight to my cock. "Tell him, Fallon. Tell him all about Ryan."

I move my hands to her waist and inch her closer. I despise turtlenecks, even as tight as this one is around her.

It accentuates her breasts but makes it impossible to kiss her anywhere but right below her ear, which is where I brush my lips.

A soft sigh falls from her lips as she tilts her head. My hands graze her thighs, my thumbs kneading the skin right beneath where her skirt starts. "You're not talking. Speak."

Her eyes fall closed when I pull her earlobe between my teeth. "Um, Thomas, I…" Another sigh. "I went to dinner with Ryan last night. He sent m-more signed copies of Alyssa's book." She fists my shirt and holds me close to her, pure ecstasy in the way her face relaxes.

I don't think it'd take much to make her come.

"But I think…" She twists just enough to turn her head toward me, opening her eyes to stare into mine. "I think Fitz got a little jealous of him. He showed up to dinner."

My mouth draws into a straight line. "I don't get jealous, Fallon. Especially not of lesser men."

She realizes she sparked an unwelcome emotion in me when a slight, triumphant grin stretches across her mouth. Using her free hand, she places her palm against my cheek. "I was happy to see you, Fitz."

I don't realize my breathing has increased until she slides her hand down to my chest. As easily as she's let me control her so far, she was able to take me down a notch with a simple sentence. All I want to do is now regain the power. "Hang up," I command.

"Thomas, I'll call you in the morning. I hope Ansel feels better soon." She listened to his reply before ending the call and placing her phone on the counter. "Fitz, I—"

I don't let her finish, quickly cupping her chin in my hand and pressing my lips to hers. The kiss is slow at first, tentative, but as soon as she wraps her arms around my neck, something inside me shifts, and I kiss her with an unexpected passion.

Her hand threads through my hair, sending shivers down my spine. The kiss turns urgent and all-consuming, our bodies nothing more than limbs stuck together. I can feel the heat between us, the way our bodies seem to magnetize to each other, and I can't pull away. More than that, I don't want to pull away. But I do want *more*.

My hands return to her thighs and slide beneath her skirt. I don't even need to pause for her permission because she automatically gives it to me, shifting her hips to allow me to locate the waistband of her tights and pull them down. I use one arm to wrap around her waist and the other to drag my thumb across the crease of her thigh. "You were bare under these all day," I say hoarsely, immediately resuming the kiss.

I'm suddenly driven by lust without logic.

I drag her hips closer, spreading her legs further apart. She whimpers into my mouth when my thumb moves to her clit, and I return it with a groan into hers. Like I expected, she's soaked. Making her come will only take two minutes tops.

I might be moving too quickly. My thoughts are already a mess, warring between need and coherence, but I want to be the one to release the tension she's always carrying.

Slowly, achingly since my cock is straining against my jeans, I slide one finger inside her. Her lips part when she breaks from me, her head falling back. I take the chance to look between our bodies, watching my hand as it disappears in a rhythm beneath her skirt. Needy for more, she tries to chase my hand, but it's pointless. I'll decide how quickly she comes.

"You were happy to see me," I repeat her earlier words back to her, unsure of why that matters to me. But I recall the excitement in her voice when she called my name at dinner last night, the elation in her smile when I joined them.

"Yes," she says with a breath, urging me to move faster when she presses her hips against my hand. "Fitz——"

"I know what you want, Fallon." I pause to kiss her again, grinning against her mouth when I add another finger. Her moan is swallowed by me when my tongue tangles with hers.

Moving my arm from around her waist to twist her braid around my wrist, I anticipate her next move. Because when I add my palm to apply pressure against her clit, she tries to break away from me to throw her head back, but I want her to come while her lips are against mine.

"Fitz," she breathes, trying to readjust and gain space to gather herself, but too high to fight too much.

"Come, Fallon," I whisper before sliding my tongue between her lips again.

And she does. She completely shatters in my hold, her entire body tensing as she comes on my fingers, then melting in my arms as the shockwaves ripple through her.

I don't stop moving my hand until I'm certain she's finished, then steady it to refocus entirely on our kiss. I could make her come again. Fuck, I could even ask her to get down on her knees to suck my cock, but I can't take too much too soon. I need to leave her wanting more from me. I've played this game before with women I wanted repeats with, but with Fallon… I don't feel like a player in a game I invented. Instead, I feel like I'm in the crowd, unsure of what comes next. I need her to want more from me because *I* want more.

She locks her legs around my waist and holds me close to her, already wanting exactly that: *more*. She isn't making this an easy decision for me, but I remove my fingers from her pussy and break our kiss to slide them into my mouth.

Fuck, she's sweet. And fuck, I want my tongue to experience what my hand just did. I want her to ride my face more than I want to take my next breath.

She blinks as she watches me, her lips red and full from the intensity of our kiss. "Fitz," she murmurs, wrapping her fingers around my wrist. She's high on lust.

"Fallon," I reply, placing my hands on her thighs to remove her legs from around me. This will sting her. Women like Fallon want romance. She might be hoping I'll stay. "It's late."

She glances at the clock on the microwave behind me, undoubtedly thinking of a way to argue with me, but I'm already aware it's past midnight. "I didn't realize," she mutters, refusing to look at me.

I brush my thumb across her swollen bottom lip, drawing her attention back to me. "I'll see you in a few hours." To ease the rejection she might feel, I kiss her gently. Softly. And I fight the urge to stay. "Thank you for the sandwich."

That draws a small smile from her. "You're welcome."

I step away from her with some hesitation, retrieve my jacket from the barstool, and wait for her to slide off the counter and readjust her skirt so she can walk me to the door. I want to carry her to the bedroom, lie her down, and kiss her until she falls asleep, which is an unsettling feeling for me. Typically, I have no problem leaving after intimacy.

"I could, um…" She gestures to my pants. "Help."

I can't help but laugh as I shrug my jacket on, nodding. "I have no doubt that you could, but the memory of you coming on my fingers will be enough when I jerk off tonight."

She gnaws on the corner of her bottom lip to stifle a shy grin. "Great. I'm happy I could be of assistance."

I playfully pull on her braid. "Until tomorrow, little tragedy."

Her nose wrinkles at the nickname, but she leans up and kisses the corner of my mouth. "Goodnight, Fitz."

As she closes the door and leaves me standing in the hallway, I stare blankly ahead. *She was happy to see me.* At dinner with another man, Fallon was happy to see me.

*fallon*

So, that happened last night. I might've longed for physical contact between us but didn't anticipate more than a kiss last night. I'd be lying if I said I didn't purposely extend our night by going into the grocery store. I had food at home I could've made. I wanted an excuse to invite him upstairs without looking like I was expecting too much. But I received much more than a kiss, and now I'm unsure how to behave around him. He greeted me this morning normally, with a simple good morning and a charming grin, and then he went straight to work. Anticipating shipments today, he showed up in gray sweatpants and a navy shirt that clings to his muscles, which hasn't helped steady my heart rate at all.

Similar to him, and because I'm exhausted from our late night and working extra hard these last two days, I'm in black leggings and an oversized sweatshirt. I showered, at least, and brushed my hair so I currently don't look completely unkempt. But me in sweats versus him? No contest. I'd choose him any day.

We've had so much foot traffic today that we haven't had a chance to talk—not that I'm expecting a conversation about what happened last night. I'd rather not talk about it. I'd like a repeat, but I won't pressure him. Oh god, what's the protocol for things like this? I haven't dated anyone since college. Is that what I'm doing with Fitz? I don't know what to expect from a guy who fingered me after I made him a kickass sandwich. Do I invite him over again tonight?

Was it a one-time thing? How do I know?

He brushes past me to grab a bag for a customer, his hand holding my waist on the way by. I jump slightly, lost in the thought of him and what this could mean between us. Noticing my reaction, he raises an eyebrow at me with a slight smirk. "Something on your mind, Fallon?" he inquires.

"Shut up," I mutter, ringing up another customer.

After he finishes bagging books, he stands behind me and places his arms on either side of the counter, caging me in. "Can you believe how she speaks to me?" he asks the customer I'm working with. "Awful conditions to work in."

I roll my eyes as the lady I'm checking out laughs, taking her card to run it through. "I believe I've shown you the door once before, so you can go if you're so unhappy."

His body wash envelopes me. He always smells good, but today, he smells more rugged than usual.

He doesn't move from behind me. Instead, he bags her purchases while keeping me in place. His arms are wrapped around me, even as he hands her the bag and asks if she's okay with her receipt being texted.

I laugh. "Are you doing my job for me now?"

He moves my hair off my shoulder, leaning in to whisper in my ear, "Are you implying you'd be okay if I walked out?"

I know dozens of people are in my store right now, but I can only feel him. At this moment, as far as I'm concerned, he's the only person with me. And with his chest against my back and his lips by my ear, it's impossible to focus on anything else anyway. All I can think about is how good his hand felt last night and how much more of him I want to experience. "No," I murmur, turning my head slightly into his. "But I believe you already know that."

He threads his fingers through my hair and holds me close, keeping his lips near my ear. "Would you like to hear what I did last night, Fallon?"

I can't nod because of how tight his grip is. "Please."

He hums his approval. "I jerked off with the same hand you came on. I thought of the sounds you made. I thought of how you tasted. And I said your name when I came."

*Fuck*, where did this man come from? Men I've been intimate with have tried talking like this but failed miserably. It was cringy and unnecessary, but when Fitz does it? His voice alone causes my stomach to do flips.

I don't realize my eyes have fallen closed until he removes himself from me completely and says with a hint of amusement in his voice, "You have customers."

I whip my head around and blush, clearing my throat as I greet the first customer in the line of five at the register. Fitz stands next to me and beckons one forward, but not before winking at me. A sinister promise for later, I hope.

---

When later approaches, we are no longer alone. Tired of being cramped in his apartment with his sick boyfriend, Thomas has joined us to unload inventory. I'm trying to behave normally, but Fitz keeps finding reasons to touch me when Thomas isn't looking. And when he isn't touching me, he's throwing me grins because he knows I can't stop thinking about everything he said earlier. I'm dying to know what he sounds like when he says my name while coming. In fact, I purposely hit him on the stomach with a book earlier to see if he'd at least groan it.

That resulted in him chasing me around the storeroom until Thomas appeared, asking exactly what was happening. Since then, we've mostly kept our distance... for the most part.

Whatever is unraveling between us, the physical chemistry between us is evident. If anything, sharing an occasional orgasm with him could help ease the stress I feel from running the store. I've shoved feelings down before. If he doesn't want anything more than being friend*ly* with benefits, I could convince myself to be okay with it. Just as long as, you know, he doesn't benefit from anyone else.

I sigh aloud from my inner monologue. The idea of sharing him is already plaguing me, and I've only had one physical encounter with him. But judging by his reaction last night when I talked to Thomas about Ryan, it doesn't seem like he's keen on sharing me.

This could be beneficial for both of us.

"Fallon," Thomas says, his eyebrow raised as he stares at me. "What's on your mind?"

I duck my head as I move a pile of books from a box to one of the storage shelves. "Um, nothing. Why?"

"Right." He stops what he's doing and comes to lean against the shelf I'm working on. "In the year I've known you, you've never not thought of *something*."

Subtlety, I glance over my shoulder. Fitz is unloading boxes from the truck just outside. I planned to eventually tell Thomas what happened anyway, and there's no time like the present. "Something happened," I whisper, shushing him when he asks me questions.

"Last night," I continue hushedly, throwing continuous

looks outside to ensure Fitz hasn't walked in. "And then today, he… said things."

Thomas wiggles his eyebrows. "Filthy things? He seems like the type."

Upon hearing that, I begin braiding my hair, twisting the end into a knot. "What do you mean?"

Thomas retrieves the pile of books from my arms and begins organizing them for me, knowing my anxious habits too well. "Fallon, please. *Look at him.* He exudes BDE. He knows what he's doing. I bet his count is… astronomical."

My mind spirals as I gnaw on my bottom lip. Astronomical? I can count the men I've been with on one hand. It wouldn't even take an entire hand. I focused on my studies in college. I wanted to graduate with honors. Not that fucking around would've slowed that down. I could've fooled around more, but I just… wasn't interested.

"Like… ten?" I squeak.

Thomas side-eyes me. "Oh, my sweet summer child."

I wonder if Fitz senses my inexperience. Is that why he left so soon last night? Was he doubting my ability to please him? No, that can't be it. He said he went home and thought of me.

"Slackers," Fitz says behind me.

I whip around, face flushed, braid falling loose. He studies me intently, cocking his head to the side. I'm sure he realizes I've been talking about him, but Thomas steps in before I start rambling about something random. "It's my fault. I was trying to coerce Fallon into going to eat dinner with me. If I have to eat one more bowl of chicken noodle soup, I'll die."

Goddamnit, Thomas. I hoped Fitz would ask me to dinner after we unloaded the boxes.

Fitz grabs a bottle of water from the package I keep on hand for delivery days and twists the cap off. "We can't let that happen. Help a man out, Fallon. I have to meet

Andrew and Jace for dinner this evening. Andrew just got in from Boston."

Maybe I shouldn't have expected to spend two nights with him in a row. We've been together practically nonstop for days. Of course, he'd rather spend time with his friends.

I decide to play it cool, though I'm pretty sure I'm experiencing my first hot flash. "Okay, but I get to choose this time."

With a sigh, Thomas finishes the box we're working on. "Fallon, we can't continue eating at Wings & Things just because you find the servers attractive."

I crinkle my nose. "That's *you*."

Thomas breaks down the box. "Oh, that's right. Wings sound great, Fallon; amazing suggestion." With a wink at Fitz and a middle finger for me, Thomas leaves us to toss the box and wait for me outside.

Leaving me alone with Fitz after what I just told him is a criminal act, especially given my disappointment for not seeing him tonight. And once Thomas returns to work, which I have a feeling will be tomorrow, Fitz won't need to be here on days we don't receive shipments.

I blow my bangs off my forehead. "I guess I'm having wings for dinner this evening."

Fitz chuckles and tosses the empty water bottle into the small trash can behind me. "Sounds like it." He produces his phone from his pocket, unlocks it, and offers it to me. "You have my number, but I don't have yours."

An obnoxiously big smile stretches across my face as I take the phone from his hand and program my information into his contacts. "Should I be expecting prank calls?"

"Nah." He slides his phone into his pocket. "Just a lot of Apple Pay requests. Those tutoring lessons of mine add up." He presses a button then flips the phone around to show me the contact photo he set for me. "I told you I'd find use for it."

I stare at the picture of me in the helmet from when we rode his bike. Then, I cringe from my smushed cheeks, and scowl. "That's it. I'm never riding with you again."

He tosses his phone on the desk, then grabs my sweatshirt and pulls me toward him. "How about... just riding *me*?"

I'm about to ask him if we can skip our plans with other people tonight to make that happen when a balled up receipt hits me on the back of the head. Thomas snaps his fingers from behind us, undoubtedly pleased he interrupted us.

"Let's *go*," he shouts.

I sigh through my nose, silently convincing myself not to kill him. "I'll consider it while I eat," I tell Fitz, raising a hand behind my back and flipping Thomas off. "Maybe."

Fitz tucks hair behind my ear. "I highly recommend it, Fallon. Don't think too hard."

As Fitz leaves me standing alone, I watch him confidently walk away, knowing I don't need to ponder the thought at all. At first opportunity, I will ride that man until I'm raw.

*fallon*

W hile we eat dinner, I fill Thomas in on everything between me and Fitz, including his most recent interaction, asking for my number. I'm trying not to read too much into that one. I'm his boss. It makes sense that he'd need my number. Thomas reminds me that Fitz has his number, though. If it was something work-related, he could just reach out to Thomas.

"I just don't like the unknown," I mutter, dipping a wing into ranch and popping it into my mouth.

"Not everything needs to be defined," Thomas replies. "When was your last relationship? Mizzou, freshman year, right? You've avoided men since then?"

I throw my napkin at him, then regret it when I realize my fingers are covered in wing sauce. "He broke my heart! I haven't been avoiding men. I just never found someone I wanted to be with. I was too busy—"

"Studying," he interrupts with a sigh. "Yeah, I've heard this story. You realize that's a bullshit excuse you hide behind, don't you? Many people socialize *and* study." He leans forward and covers my hand with his. "Your ex-boyfriend from eons ago is not why you're guarding your heart, Fallon."

"Don't," I warn gently. "I don't want to go there."

He squeezes my hand. "How much longer can you live like that? You have to face——"

"Thomas." With all the patience I can muster, I convey the seriousness of the subject he's about to broach. "I don't want to talk about it."

He holds his palms up like he's trying to prevent a rabid dog from biting him. "Fine." Picking up a piece of celery, he points it at me. "But that's why you're wanting a definition. It feels safer to you when you know what to expect."

"Stop weaponizing vegetables and change the subject."

He does. He asks me questions about my upcoming trip to California, asks if Fitz is serious about going with me, talks about how whiny Ansel is when he's ill, and then goes into how much fun his younger brother is having on his trip to Paris.

I try not to die of envy. At twenty-five, this is the time to travel and experience the world. Traveling to Europe and learning about cultures different than mine is a dream I don't have time to live. I was supposed to go to Paris after graduating from college, but… I don't finish the thought.

My phone lights up with a text, pulling me from my thoughts. The name that flashes makes me drop the wing I'm holding and reach across the table to retrieve my napkin.

How are the wings?

"He just texted me," I say, rereading the simple question five times before I respond.

Wingy.

How is your dinner?

I didn't expect to hear from him at all this evening, but he made an effort, which has admittedly excited me more than it should for a man I could hardly stand just days ago.

Loud.

Jace brought us to a Mexican restaurant
that gives you sombreros and sings to you
when it's your birthday.

A picture comes through of Andrew wearing a sombrero with a scowl on his face. Jace is next to him, holding up a frozen margarita, his mouth open like he's singing along.

I show the picture to Thomas before replying.

Is it Andrew's birthday?

No.

Jace is just a dick.

I laugh while taking a sip of my cola. As interesting as Fitz's friendship is with Jace, there does seem to be brotherly love hidden beneath their unfathomable competitiveness. They wouldn't spend so much time together if there was genuine dislike. Jace and Andrew certainly wouldn't travel here from Boston as often as they do.

I heart the picture.

I want to see the sombrero on you.

I didn't realize you were into role-play.

You'll be the matador?

I throw my head back, laughing, the scenario playing in my mind of what that would even look like.

Something to consider.

What are your plans after dinner?

Oh, god. Oh, god. "Oh, god." I show Thomas the text, trying not to jump around in my seat. "Does he want to see me? What do I say? I don't have plans."

"Don't say that," Thomas replies, watching me dance around with a bemused grimace. "Tell him you're not sure, then ask him if he has suggestions."

I send the emoji of the girl shrugging.

Have any suggestions?

How do you feel about hot chocolate?

The small cafe across from my apartment building, *Corner Brews*, is one of the best in Sanderling and is always busy. There are rarely any tables available, and even if you find one, you'll be subjected to a noisy environment and a constant chill from the door opening and closing. Shoreline Scribes partnered with them once to host a *Caffeine with your Literacy?* Day. Each location had coupons available for customers to use at either place. I offered 10% off a purchase, and Brews offered a free 12oz coffee or discount off their specialty drinks. Not that I consider them my competition, but they're probably the second most viable new business in Sanderling.

"That's a brilliant partnership," Fitz says after I explain to him how beneficial it ended up being for both businesses. "You doubled the amount of funds poured into your local economy. People are starving for the ability to support a small business. Genius, Fallon. Truly."

"Thank you," I say proudly. "The owner opened Brews shortly after I opened the store. She's a single mom. Her seven-year-old son loves to come in once a week after school and always chooses two books. It's how we met. I was happy to partner with her."

Fitz nods as he listens. "Would you say connecting with other local businesses improves your sales?"

"*Improves* them?" I wrinkle my nose in thought. "Maybe? I try to befriend the owners of local businesses strictly to support them, but maybe the relationships I build with them somehow translate into word-of-mouth customers?"

We walk across the street to my building. We ordered our hot chocolates and decided to skip the experience of trying to find a place to sit. And now, I'm trying to calm my raging heartbeat and work up the nerve to invite him upstairs.

I punch the security code into the pin pad, place my hand on the door handle, and blow out a breath. "Want to come up?" I ask, knowing I'll melt into the cement if he declines.

He doesn't pretend to contemplate. Instead, he follows me inside without a word. I'm on the top floor but always skip the elevator. He doesn't complain during the climb up four flights of stairs or seem breathless when we make it to my door. Through the tightness of his shirt today, I could see the lines of his abs. I imagine Fitz is as perfect underneath his clothes as he is when you can only see his face.

"Did Jace and Andrew go back to Boston?"

Fitz follows me inside and places his cup on the small table in the entry to remove his jacket. "No, they're staying at my place this weekend. That's why I didn't invite you over."

Staying at his place? Because we're a high-traffic tourist area, Sanderling isn't a cheap place to live, especially if you have more than one bedroom. My one-bedroom apartment works perfectly for me, but if I had someone staying here? That would be a tight squeeze. "I've noticed the three of you are attached at the hip."

"Don't I fucking know it," he mutters, tossing his jacket over the arm of my couch.

I shrug off my jacket and hang it up in the very tiny coat closet by the front door. "Was it not like that when you lived in Boston? It doesn't seem like they're used to being away from you."

He cocks his head while reading the titles of the books I have stacked on the mantle. "It was. When I travel, they're there. When I go anywhere, they're there." A combination of a sigh and a laugh leaves him. "Jace's fucking ringtone for me and Andrew is that song from *The Hangover*."

"The one Zach Galifianakis sings?"

"The very one."

"That's adorable." I point to the switch beside the fireplace. "Why don't you flip that on? That hot chocolate wasn't enough to warm me up. That'll make it feel like a sauna."

Instead of doing as I ask, he gives me a knowing grin. "We don't need that to warm up, Fallon."

I swallow. "Oh?" I'd be lying if I said this wasn't what I was hoping for by inviting him up. But having him here now, already having crossed that line with him, and with Thomas' warning about Fitz's body count still living rent-free in my mind, I'm suddenly questioning everything.

Should I light candles? Put on something more revealing? I'm still in the leggings and oversized sweatshirt from work today. It's not exactly my sexiest look. Not that I even own lingerie to tease him with. I'm wholly unprepared.

"I'm not going to bite you," Fitz says softly, his voice a quiet rasp.

I glance up, caught by the teasing tone in his voice. "Then why do you look like you want to?"

He chuckles, and for a second, the tension breaks. But only for a second. The moment his eyes meet mine again, it returns, stronger this time, like we're standing on the edge of something we both know we can't turn back from.

The living room is dimly lit by the soft glow of the floor lamp, casting shadows that dance gently against the walls. The city lights outside are muted, a constant hum beneath the quiet stillness between us. I try to pretend like my heart isn't pounding in my chest. The air between us is thick, charged with something unspoken that has been building since the first time we met. Every glance, touch, and moment we share seems to pull us closer to this.

My pulse quickens, and I can't help but feel the pull toward him. Without thinking, I cross the room until I'm standing in front of him. Fitz remains still, watching me carefully, his eyes dark with desire and something deeper.

I can't think about this. I have to just let it happen. We've teased it all day. I know it's what we both want to happen. "Kiss me," I whisper.

His hands find my waist beneath the sweatshirt, warm against my skin, and for a long moment, we simply stand here, the tension thick between us. Is he reconsidering?

Then, as if the dam breaks, he pulls me into him, his lips crashing against mine with a force that leaves me breathless. The kiss is deep and urgent as if he's been holding back all day just as much as I have. His hands roam to the back of my neck, pulling me closer, and I melt into him, my hands threading into his hair and tugging him closer.

His lips move against mine with an intensity that makes

my head spin. A surge of heat explodes between us like a spark igniting a fire I'm only now realizing has been there.

I moan softly, the sound barely escaping my throat as his hands slide down my back, pulling me against him, feeling the hard planes of his chest against the softness of mine.

"I want you," he whispers against my lips, his breath ragged. "Fuck, Fallon, I want to feel all of you."

I don't know how to respond, how to put into words how my body is reacting to him, or how every part of me seems to hum with the need for more. Instead, I kiss him harder, my lips parting as his tongue gently presses against mine. The world around us seems to fall away, leaving just the two of us lost in each other.

He guides us toward the couch, the back of my knees hitting the cushions as the heat of his body presses against mine. His hands move to the hem of my sweatshirt, slipping it over my head in one smooth motion, exposing the soft skin of my torso. I shiver as the cool air of the room meets my skin, but the warmth of his hands quickly replaces it, his fingertips grazing over my bare skin, sending electric jolts through my body.

"Keep me burning," I plead.

"Fallon," he breathes, his voice low and rough as his lips trail down my neck, leaving a trail of fire wherever they touch.

I arch into him, a gasp escaping my lips as the pulse between my thighs intensifies. My hands move to his shirt, tugging it over his head, my fingers tracing the defined muscles of his chest as I marvel at the way he feels beneath my fingertips. His arms are covered in tattoos, the beautiful markings in black ink making me want to color them in. Paint him mine.

"Are you sure?" Fitz asks, his voice is hushed but thick

with desire. He pauses, his forehead resting against mine as his breath mingles with mine. "You can tell me to stop."

"Don't stop. Do the opposite," I say hurriedly.

I capture his lips with mine again, pulling him back down on top of me. I don't want more hesitation or doubt or *thinking*. I want him in the most primal way.

The moment his lips meet mine again, it's like a floodgate opens. His hands move with a sense of urgency, peeling off my clothes until I'm left with nothing but the warmth of his touch and the overwhelming pull between us. Every inch of my skin feels alive under his touch.

The emotions running through me are foreign, but I welcome them with open arms. It's the most I've truly let myself feel in a year. He's settling my mind.

That should terrify me.

But all I want is more.

*hayes*

I wasn't planning for this to happen so soon after arriving at her apartment. I was okay to talk to her, maybe start a movie, play a fucking board game, I don't know. But she looked so damn appetizing in the dim glow of her apartment, nervous and fidgeting. She's intimidated by me—that much I've gathered. And judging by how quickly she came for me last night, I think she's out of practice in the sex department.

She was so relaxed and playful at work today, and I take all the credit for it. I enjoy flirting with her... distracting her. She's been so focused on growing her business for a year that she's forgotten what it's like to feel good. It's why she's so active every evening after work when she works out. She's chasing that high, but I'm about to provide one for her that she'll never be able to replicate on her own.

She kicks off her shoes to allow me to yank her leggings down. But when she leans forward to find the waistband of my pants, I grab her wrists to stop her. "Not so fast, Fallon." Leaning back on my shins, I lick my lips while admiring her body. I've imagined what she looks like beneath her clothing hundreds of times now, but I didn't do her justice.

She's perfect. Her breasts are full and busting out of her bra, her nipples perky and swollen. Her hair has fallen over her chest and stomach, but I can make out the soft lines of her abs from her nights of Pilates. But her thighs are exactly what I want at the moment.

"Remove your thong, Fallon."

Hesitation ripples through her for a second, but then it's returned with a defiant little nod—something she probably doesn't think I noticed. Her breasts bounce when she stands and shimmies out of her thong, but I grab it before she can kick it away and bring it to my nose.

Fuck, it's only been twenty-four hours, but the way she smells gets me hard. I toss her thong on top of my shirt. "That's a good girl," I murmur, dropping to my knees to kiss down her stomach. "I'm going to fuck you tonight." I drag my teeth across her left hipbone. "First with my tongue…" then her right hipbone. "And then I'm going to bend you over this couch and make you come on my cock."

She's already panting from the slightest touch. I glance up at her. Does she always get worked up easily, or does she genuinely want me this badly? "Fallon, have you ever been fucked?"

Her hands find my shoulders, her eyes glazed from lust as she watches me skim my teeth across her stomach. "Not since college," she whispers timidly.

With a chuckle, I shake my head. "No, Fallon. I didn't ask if you've ever been screwed. I asked if you've ever been fucked. Has a man ever made you come so hard that you can't catch your breath? Has he ever made you feel so good that you were wet just from thinking about him?"

"Um, yes," she squeaks. "Today."

*Fuck.* All I did was finger her.

This is a dangerous game I'm playing. If she's already aching for me just from the bare minimum, what will she be like after I fuck her? I could awaken the beast in her.

I don't acknowledge what she admitted. Instead, I lower to the floor on my back as she watches me in confusion. This will be another first for her, I assume. "Straddle my head."

"*Oh*," she says when the realization hits, a bashful grin spreading across her mouth. Of course, she knows. Fallon is a reader. I've been with enough women to know what's in their books, especially when they've read something they want to try. But if Fallon hasn't been with anyone since college, I have a feeling she'll experience *a lot* of firsts with me.

Lowering to her knees, she straddles my chest first, then timidly scoots closer to my head. I'm anxious to eat and am dwindling on patience, so I grab her waist with my hands and drag her forward. She releases a surprised gasp, instinctively trying to slow down, but I hold a firm grip on her.

Even as dim as it is in the living room, her pussy looks delectable and pink and needs to be riding my tongue.

"I don't think—"

"Good, don't think," I interrupt. "I don't want to chase your pussy, Fallon. I want to be smothered by it. Sit."

As she drops to my mouth, my hands slide from her waist to cup her ass, and I begin to feast. She's just as sweet as I remember and so wet that my tongue is immediately covered. I breathe in every inch of her pussy, high from lust, drowning in desire, and so goddamn thirsty for more.

I feel each movement of her body as she jerks and arches, not used to someone eating her this way. I squeeze her ass in my hands, urging her to move her hips. I want access to as much of her as possible, and I can make her come harder if she just relaxes and allows me control.

I drag my teeth down her clit to recenter her and grab her attention.

"Fuck," she rasps, lifting her hips.

"Fallon, relax. Let me take care of you." I lock eyes with her, convinced I have a goddess hovering above me. Her hair is cascading down her chest and covering her breasts, and I swear her bright green eyes are glowing in the faint light. "I want you to ride my face the same way you'd ride my cock."

"I don't want to suffocate you…"

"*I* want you to suffocate me," I assure her. "Fallon, I'm hard from tasting you. I want you to come all over my tongue. You taste so fucking good. Ride me. Use me to feel good."

After a small nod, she allows me to pull her back down. I suck her clit between my lips, my cock jolting when she whimpers my name. Just to hear it again, I repeat the motion before sliding my tongue inside her. Leaning forward enough to thread her hands through my hair, she finally starts to roll her hips against my tongue. Fuck *yes*.

Her movements are unsteady as she tries to find her rhythm, and I use my hands on her ass to guide her into an anchored flow. Her breathy moans fill the room, her skin slicking from the beads of sweat forming.

She's so close. Her tempo has increased, and her breathing is uneven. She's whimpering and arching her back, her grip on my hair tightening. I want to encourage her, but I'm too content with my face buried in her pussy, and slightly hoping she'll continue delaying so I can stay right where I am.

But when her legs begin to shake, and her pussy tightens around my tongue, my hold on her strengthens. I don't want her trying to pull away when she comes. "Fitz," she rasps. "Fitz, Fitz, I'm going to come… oh, god."

I groan as she does exactly that. She gushes on my

tongue, coming in waves, her pussy pulsing and quivering. I drink from her like a man dying of thirst. Unrelenting.

Her body relaxes, but I don't let her move. Instead, I suck her clit into my mouth again. No woman has ever made me want to draw two orgasms like this, but I'm not ready to be done yet. I feel as if I've been starved for her. I'm desperate to be inside her, but I want her chanting my name again.

"Fitz, I can't…" She moans then, because yes. She can.

My hands slide up to wrap around her waist, and she arches into my touch. I want her completely dependent on me for her pleasure. I want her wet enough that my cock will slide right inside her. I want nothing slowing us down when I fuck her. She starts to rock again, more controlled now. She knows exactly what she needs from me to make herself come.

It only takes a couple minutes before she's coming again, crying my name like it's a final prayer. But she's the one taking me to heaven and back while I'm desperate to drag her to hell.

I allow her to slow this time, soaking in the last moment of my face being buried in her pussy. But the second she raises, I'm out from between her legs and up, untying the knot of my waistband and shedding my pants. She's leaning back on her heels, her head tilted back while she tries to catch her breath.

"You did so good," I assure her, licking my lips. I retrieve a condom from my wallet and tear open the package with my teeth while holding my cock in my hand. "So, so good."

She looks at me over her shoulder, biting her bottom lip as her eyes fall on my cock. They widen ever so slightly. "My dildo isn't that big," she whispers.

The image of her fucking herself paints a picture in my mind, only adding to my growing desperation of feeling her around me. "Fucking yourself won't ever be the same, Fallon." I stroke myself once. "Only I can make you come as hard as you did. As you will. Stand up."

On shaky legs, she does as she's told. She was meant to submit. She just needed someone she could trust. She's so used to being in control. But here with me, she won't be.

"I'm on the pill," she informs me. "I want…"

When she trails off, I cock my head. "Say it."

"I don't want the condom."

*Fuck.* "You want me to fuck you raw?"

That does surprise me. For someone who's always in her head, wanting me to fuck her without protection is her treading into the unknown. And I have to blindly trust that she's on the pill. I'd refuse them outright if it was anyone else, like someone who knows who I am and my net worth. But Fallon has no idea who I am. She just wants the version of me she's come to know.

"I can show you if you'd like," she says, referring to her method of birth control. "But I want… to feel you."

She doesn't need to prove anything.

I toss the condom on the floor and beckon her closer. "Then come here, Fallon. Feel me."

She draws closer and wraps her hand around my cock, pulling a soft moan from me. And when she begins jerking me off, she looks up at me from underneath her long lashes and asks, "Is this what you did last night while thinking of me?"

I close my hand around hers and slow the pace. "Just like this, Fallon." I close my eyes as my head rolls back. "Fuck, just like that. All I could see was you coming over and over."

"Didn't you mention bending me over?"

A low chuckle rumbles through my chest. "Needy girl." She fists my length, earning another satisfied groan from me. "Bend over the arm of the couch, Fallon."

I replace her hand with my own, resuming the pace she kept while she saunters toward the couch. As she wants, I watch the sway of her hips. If I was meaner, I'd make myself come right now and spray her ass, but I want to feel her pussy around me. I am relieved to see her more relaxed than when we started, but now I want to ensure she feels nothing but me for the rest of the week.

She bends forward over the arm of her sofa and stretches her arms out straight, her fingers curling around the cushion. She's already bracing herself. I stand behind her and admire how tight her ass looks from this position. Primed. Pure. So, I spank her hard enough for red to blossom.

She gasps and lifts her head, trying to look at me, but I lean forward and fist her hair, shoving her back down. "Trust me," I plead, aligning my cock with her entrance. "Relax."

I ease the tip inside, giving her a few seconds to adjust. "Sweet girl, I meant what I said. I need you to relax." With my free hand, I drag my finger down her spine to calm her. She's so tight, even after riding my face and coming twice. "You feel so good, Fallon. I need more."

She releases a deep breath and sinks into the couch, except she's just as desperate as I am, and presses her hips closer to me.

"Fuck," I rasp, sliding in slowly, inch by inch. "You take me so well. I wish you could see it."

She moans when I'm fully inside her, the noise muffled against the cushion, but she's not fighting me. She's freely giving me all the power to bring her pleasure.

Anchoring my palm against her lower back, I slowly start thrusting, pulling out to the tip before gliding in again. "Did it feel good when I spanked you?" I loosen my hold just enough on her hair to feel her nod. "Say it. Tell me you want it."

She twists her head to give me her side profile. A bashful smile is on her lips. "Spank me, Fitz."

As I thrust into her, I do just that. She presses her ass into me instinctively, giving me another inch. Fuck, I won't last much longer. I've edged myself too long. "Say it again."

One of her hands disappears underneath her, and I watch as she slides it to her pussy. "Spank me again, Fitz. Harder."

"Fallon, are you rubbing your clit?" I reach underneath her and remove her hand, then spank her again, admiring the handprint starting to form. "You want to touch yourself?" I pull out of her. "Lay down on your side."

She whimpers from my absence but crawls fully onto the couch and twists on her left side. I lay behind her and grab her leg, lifting it to rest against my hip, then slide my cock back inside her. "Then do it where I can watch." I prop up on my elbow before I start thrusting. "Touch yourself, baby."

She slides her hand between her legs, using her middle finger against her clit. The vision is euphoric. Her head is against my chest, her back arched, and her ass pressed against me, and she's rubbing herself in tempo with my thrusts.

"Fitz," she whines, her lips parting and eyes closing.

"Louder," I growl, increasing my pace. "I want everyone in this building to hear how hard I make you come." I look between our bodies, watching myself disappear inside her over and over. "Fuck, Fallon, I'm going to fill you up."

"Oh, god," she moans, the sound of her finger moving on her clit nearly my undoing. "Fitz, I'm going to come again."

"All over me," I plead, rocking us so hard that the cushions start sliding off. I'm positive she'll have bruises on her hips from how tightly I'm holding onto her.

I dive in and capture her lips with mine when she turns her head toward me. Our sounds are muffled together, the sound of our bodies moving together filling the room, and when she slides her tongue into my mouth, I can't hold back anymore, and neither can she. We come in tandem.

My visions blurs as a cold sweat overtakes me, my arms wrapping around her to tether myself back to reality. She's breathless and shaking but still kissing me. I twist to lay on my back and adjust her to rest against my chest, pulling a blanket from the top of the couch to cover us with. I'm usually great about aftercare, but we both need a few moments to recover. "Are you okay?" I ask, rubbing her back.

She lifts her head with a lazy, satisfied grin. "Amazing."

With a grin, I tuck a strand of hair behind her ear. "You did so well, my little tragedy. Thank you for trusting me."

She doesn't utter a word. Instead, she stares into my eyes for a few seconds before she inches forward. And then, she kisses me. It's long and slow. It's sweet. And an unfamiliar feeling sprouts in my chest.

## *fallon*

We fell asleep on the couch until he woke up at two in the morning. He kissed me on the temple before leaving, taking his warmth with him. I fell asleep until my alarm went off at seven, and my body screamed through a shower. Every muscle is sore. I don't even feel like I did much last night, but I long to lie down and sleep some more with each movement. But the pain is worth every orgasm he gave me last night. I haven't felt this relaxed in a very long time, though if he walked through my door right now and demanded we go again, I'd probably cry.

But fuck, he felt good. It's unfair that a man who looks like him is also some kind of sex wizard, but I'll reap the benefits. As long as no one else is. No, we're not going there. He doesn't owe me anything. We never drew lines. I should've. My behavior lately is very unlike me. I always plan and plot, know what to expect, and rarely deviate. His ability to turn my mind off is both disarming and scary.

And poor Thomas gets to hear all about it today.

I settled on one of my many bookish spirit jerseys and jeans. My legs are stiff, but I haven't had time to do laundry, so I don't have a pair of clean leggings. If I made enough time to shop for necessities, as I have been spending time with Fitz lately, I might have more to eat and wear.

'*It's a race, not a marathon,*' my father used to tell me when I'd take life a little *too* seriously. But how can I do anything but that when trying to build something lasting and not focus so much on my past life before coming here? If I'm constantly running, I'll never have to stop for a breath.

I arrive later at the store than usual. Thomas' car is already in the lot, and I do not doubt I'll be questioned on how he arrived earlier than me. I don't think that's ever happened. But when I try to open the front door, I can't. We rarely have anyone trying to enter the store before we open, so keeping the door locked is unusual for him.

I search for my keys in my bag, only to be greeted a moment later by Thomas… blocking my way in.

"Move, clown." I try to shove past him unsuccessfully.

"Good morning, sunshine." He holds the door semi-closed, so I can't sneak by. "You're off today. You have a massage in an hour, so you better scurry along."

My brow wrinkles in confusion. "Did you hit your head on something this morning? I don't have a massage."

"Oh, you do." He shows me his calendar on his phone. *Fallon, 9:30AM—Massage with Brandy.* "I booked it last night." He produces his car keys from his pocket. "Shoo."

I shove his hand away. "You're cracked. I can't leave you here by yourself all day, Thomas."

Thomas grins. "You're not. I told you she'd need convincing." He steps aside, but not enough for me to rush in.

Instead, Fitz takes his place. He props his arm up on the doorframe and hovers above me like a fucking *god*. "Good morning, little tragedy. How was your night?"

I lick my lips as the events from last night replay in my

mind for the hundredth time this morning. "Eventful." I want to kiss him, but would that be weird? We're not dating. I mean, the man had his face in my pussy last night, but heaven forbid I greet him with a kiss because *that* would be too much. "Have you started conspiring with Thomas now?"

Fitz shrugs too nonchalantly for my taste. "He texted me last night. I didn't see it until I left your place this morning."

"Until you left where?!" Thomas shouts from behind him.

I close my eyes with a sigh. "Well, you set yourself up for a day of questioning, and he's great at wearing people down."

Thomas reappears behind Fitz. "I'm reconsidering everything. I need the details. I don't think President Grant is the best candidate for oversharing."

I bounce on my toes excitedly. "Good. Let me in."

With an eye roll, Thomas shakes his head. "I was lying. Fallon, you haven't had a day off since your last trip to California almost *a year ago*. We've got this. I'm tired of seeing you in the same outfits every week. Relax. Shop."

I should be excited and grateful that they're both willing to handle the store so that I can have a day to myself. But I also don't want to spend the day alone with just me and my thoughts. What a terrifying idea.

"He's right," Fitz says softly. "You've earned this, Fallon."

I can find enough things to do to not allow time for too much thinking. I could even nap. "Okay," I say meekly.

Thomas practically hurls his car keys at me. "We'll allow you back this evening if it's just eating at you that much." He winks at me. "You've got this, Fallon." Then he disappears to hopefully finish opening the registers.

Fitz taps his finger under my chin. "It'll be okay, Fallon.

You need to trust us. The store will still be standing tonight."

I don't like when someone guarantees something they can't control. I could think of a hundred scenarios that would result in the store falling apart while I'm gone. But the idea of a massage and nap sounds better by the second.

Fitz steps outside and closes the door behind him. "Come on, I'll walk you to the car." He holds out his arm for me to grab. "I can't allow you to linger on the sidewalk all day."

I snort as he leads me away from the store. "Surely you'd eventually take pity on me and let me inside."

He shakes his head. "Nope. You need to learn boundaries, Fallon, and that includes with yourself. I understand your need to be involved every moment, but you will eventually burn out if you keep going like this."

"I'm trying to build something—"

"You've *built* something," he interrupts. "You're one of the most influential small businesses in Sanderling. That won't change because you take a day to yourself sometimes. Even CEOs of major corporations need a day off."

"Unfortunately, I don't have access to that kind of funds to guarantee longevity like a major corp." I release him as I become defensive. "I have to work for everything this store is."

I get two steps ahead of him before I'm pulled back and spun around to walk backward. He keeps his arms locked around me. "I realize that, but you must also look at everything you have accomplished instead of constantly chasing the next step. Sometimes, there isn't one yet."

"I have a next step," I argue, trying to free myself. "I'm just waiting to hear back from someone."

He pins me against the car and cups my chin to hold my gaze. "Breathe. I'm not your enemy, Fallon." He gently presses his lips against mine. "The massage is only an hour.

I'm going to call and have it extended. Once you're relaxed and have forgiven me, text me."

He releases me all at once and starts walking away, and stubbornly, I want to get in the car and leave. I don't know what his father does or Fitz's work background, but he doesn't know the challenges I've faced in getting to where I am. Countless nights of no sleep and worry, multiple trips to book conventions, having to flirt with people I don't want to flirt with to build relationships.

But then, I realize I'm right. He doesn't know what I've faced. And taking that out on him isn't fair.

"Fitz," I say.

He stops and turns.

"That kiss was too short."

He returns instantly and kisses me deeply, our tongues entwining and moving together so familiarly. He balances his hands on my waist, my arms wrap around his neck, and we stay locked in a passionate embrace as moments pass. Neither of us moves to part from the other, even as my lips swell from the kiss.

I jolt when my phone buzzes in my back pocket and pulls me from my euphoria. Fitz is the one to slip it out of my jeans, looking over his shoulder once he sees the name on the screen. Thomas is standing in the doorway with his arms thrown up. "Let's go!" he shouts from across the street.

I can't help but laugh, dipping my head to press my forehead against Fitz's chest while he chuckles. But he lifts my chin and kisses me again, softer and quicker this time. "I meant what I said, Fallon. Text me when you're done."

I drag my knuckles down his jawline. "I will."

As I watch him cross the lot back toward the store, I take three deep breaths and repeat Thomas' words aloud.

"I've got this."

## *fallon*

I pace the inside of the lighthouse, trying to steady my breathing. In, out, in, out, three at a time. I brace against the wall, letting the cool stone pierce my palms and spread through my body. The massage was needed and incredible. I fell asleep after only a few moments. The masseuse played soothing music, used lavender-scented lotion, and didn't press too hard. But then I woke up, no longer fatigued from the night before and unable to calm racing thoughts.

I'm alone often, especially at night, but I always have something to do. I'll go to Pilates or out with Thomas. I'll stop by the cafe and chat with the owner or visit local businesses. I'll spend all night ordering inventory or planning more trips to conventions. I fill my time because it's what I've planned to do. I have a strict schedule to prevent moments like these from happening.

My phone buzzes in my back pocket. After grabbing it, I sink to the floor, wiping tears from my cheeks. I don't say anything when I answer because he somehow always knows. "Fallon?" Thomas' voice is frantic on the other end. "Why does your location show you in the water? Are you drowning? Where are you?"

"Yeah," I reply, wiping my nose on my sleeve. "You wouldn't believe the cell reception down here. Crystal clear."

"Fallon," he says gentler. "Where are you?"

"I tried," I whisper meekly.

"I know," he says with a small sigh. "I shouldn't have sprung it on you like I did. I just… wanted to help."

I lean my head back against the wall as a fresh set of tears roll down my cheeks. Fallon Madison, the grown woman unable to spend a day alone because of her intrusive thoughts, strikes again. "I'm at the lighthouse."

"The lighthouse?" he repeats. "Why did you go there?"

"Fitz brought me here once." I sniffle and wipe my tears again. "It just felt like the safest place. I didn't want to go home, and I didn't want to disappoint you by coming back."

"Fallon Madison, don't you ever say that again."

"Okay, I'm sorry," I squeak, one tear away from becoming a puddle on the floor.

"I'll be right back," Thomas says to someone—I assume Fitz—and is quiet until the storeroom door closes. "Put me on speaker and open your Notes."

I do as he says. "Okay."

"Write down what you need to do for the next few hours. Make a checklist for yourself, Fallon. You need groceries, right? But you also need clothes. Start with thrifting."

I type the name of my favorite thrift store, followed by the name of the larger supermarket close by.

"That'll fill two hours." I hear him typing on the keyboard. "There's a Pilates class a half hour after that."

I add that to my schedule.

"After Pilates, go home and shower, then return to the

store." The office chair squeaks as he leans back. "You can close tonight, then we'll invite Fitz to dinner with us."

I take a deep breath and stare at the new checklist. I have all my time accounted for until the store closes. "Thank you."

"And please text Fitz. He keeps checking his phone."

I laugh through a breathy sniffle. "I didn't think texting him during my breakdown would be very attractive."

"Stay on the phone with me until you're in the car."

I nod while I stand. "I love you, you know."

"Christ," he mutters. "You fucking better."

---

I make it to Pilates five minutes before class starts. It's been so long since I thrifted, and I went a little overboard and bought too much, but I found many cute pieces, like a vintage Kansas City Chiefs pullover. Don't ask me how it ended up in Sanderling, New Hampshire, but I took it as a sign that I needed it. As a kid, we'd sit in front of our television every time they played. My dad spent years trying to talk my mom into buying season tickets.

Did you buy sandwich ingredients?

I smile at Fitz's text. He hasn't stopped texting me since I told him I would shop before Pilates. He sent me a picture earlier of Thomas flipping off the camera. According to him, everything at the store is running smoothly, though I doubt either would be honest with me if it wasn't.

I'm going to make you an anchovy sub.

I'm allergic to anchovies.

> Oh. What will I do with all these anchovies, then?

I lied. I'm not. But I'll help you locate a trash can.

> Such chivalry.

> Class is starting, gtg.

Send a picture first.

I sink back on my shins, snap a picture in the mirror, send it, and then slide my phone into my gym bag.

---

After an hour passes and class ends, I lay on the floor and pant. It's only been a few days since my last class, but Fitz has done an excellent job of working my muscles into spasms, so to say I'm sore all over again is an understatement. I'm also positive I can't move. My instructor, Andy, lowers his hand toward me. "Did I finally break you?"

I grab his hand and hoist myself up. "I can't entirely give you all the credit, but you certainly didn't help."

Andy has been my instructor since I signed up. He co-owns the studio with his wife, but he's the tamest of the two. I tried taking her class once and almost fainted.

"You've improved since your first class six months ago," he says, helping me gather my things. "You haven't been here the last few nights, though."

"I know." I give him an apologetic shrug. "I'm..." Dating someone? Benefitting from multiple orgasms? Making out with the hottest man I've ever seen? And that includes seeing Pedro Pascal at a restaurant once in Los Angeles. I called Thomas when that happened, and he encouraged me to introduce myself to him. I absolutely did not.

"I met someone," I say. Yeah. I met someone. That's how I'll classify whatever this is with Fitz until I have a more solid answer. "He's been occupying my nights lately."

Andy beams. "Hey! That's great, Fallon."

I nod as I fish my phone out of my bag. "Yeah, he's…" I trail off when I notice I have four texts from Fitz. I swipe up quickly to open them, anticipating him telling me that the store caught fire and was engulfed in flames.

> Fuck.
>
> That's what you're wearing?
>
> Don't go home and shower.
>
> Come straight here.

I can't tell by the tone of his texts if he's upset or horny. Maybe both. I'm not wearing much more than the night he bumped into me outside. I have a long-sleeved, cropped compression shirt and spandex shorts. I suppose I'm showing a lot of skin, but I knew I'd sweat a lot this time.

"He's waiting for me," I finish before saying goodbye to Andy and replying to Fitz.

> I'm gross. I'm covered in sweat.

> Even better. See you soon.

---

I didn't shower, but I did pull my sweats out of my gym bag and put them on over my workout clothes. I'm not about to walk into my store half-naked, no matter who asks. I tried brushing my hair as best I could, but it was matted to my scalp from the sweat and ended up in a messy bun on top of my head. And thank god I packed spray deodorant.

I'm pleased to find the store's front door unlocked. I'm tempted to change the locks so Thomas can't prevent me from entering again, but he'd still find a way.

I wait by the door as Fitz bags for the last customer. He's chatting with her about something, and she's nodding her head so hard that I'm positive she's going to get a headache, but I can't help but smile. She's enamored by him. Aside from his looks, his mysterious aura is enough for any woman to want to know more.

He looks up and catches me watching him, then grins. The customer turns and walks toward me with flushed cheeks, swinging her bag by her side like she's the happiest woman in the world after just a simple interaction with him.

God, if we ever become anything more, I'll need to get used to women wanting him.

I open the door for her. "Have a great night!"

Her smile widens. "Goodnight, Fallon!"

Locking the door behind her, I release a deep breath. Something about being in my store feels safe. I can be myself here—the girl who's always read too many books.

"Did you return my car in one piece?"

I flinch when Thomas sneaks up behind me and puts his hand in the front pocket of my hoodie to retrieve his keys. "I'm going to put gas in the car and pick up Ansel. Text me where you want to eat for dinner."

Instead of responding, I wrap my arms around his chest. Without his phone call at the lighthouse, I'm positive I'd still be there, paralyzed by anxiety. His arms enclose around me, and he presses his lips to the top of my head. We don't exchange words because they're unneeded. Ever since I met Thomas, he's just understood me. He's saved me from many panic attacks and has a sixth sense of my emotions. I'm not overly spiritual, but I do believe a higher entity knew I needed him in my life.

When we finally let go, I promise to text him.

When he's gone, I walk toward Fitz, who is sitting on the counter and waiting for me. "Do you want to go to dinner with us tonight? I'll even let you choose."

He says nothing. Just watches me approach.

"Thank you for doing this today, by the way." I twist my hands nervously. He's staring at me like a predator would watch its prey. "It was your day off. You didn't have to."

"I know," he says.

I clear my throat and pause just before him. There's an undeniable tension between us, but it's purely physical. We're like two moths drawn to a burning fire. Every time we're near each other, it's explosive and all-consuming.

"I guess I should start closing—"

"Remove your sweats, Fallon."

I whisper, "Why?"

With his hand around my throat, he yanks me closer. The longing and desire in his gaze sets me aflame, but his cool exterior keeps me on edge. And that's the balance never struck between us. It's never one or the other; it is always everything all at once. It's flames and shards of ice, combining and combusting. And I am always the product of what it produces—a puddle of ashes, embers, and thirst.

Instead of pulling away as I would with anyone else, I find myself inching closer. "Because," he says, "I'm going to fuck you right here."

# *hayes*

Fallon's eyes widen, and then she glances over her shoulder at the windows of her shop. Anyone could walk past and see what I plan to do to her, and I'd encourage it. Let them watch me defile the innocent, naive bookshop owner they've all come to love and admire. Watch how she moves for me. Watch how she comes for me. Take a front-row seat and witness how quickly she's falling for me. I didn't anticipate how simple it'd be to earn her trust, nor did I realize how easily they'd let me into how this store runs. I've gathered information quickly.

Yet the way she looks at me, how she talks to me, the stubborn way she argues with almost everything I say is just as addicting as how quickly she's let me in.

"Fallon, do as I said."

I don't know what happened to her today or why Thomas was so worried about her. I know she went to the lighthouse. I heard her tell him I brought her there once and that being there makes her feel safe. And I know there's something about her past that she isn't telling me.

I know I want to unravel her.

I want to be the black ink poisoning her.

With trembling hands, most likely from nerves, Fallon grabs the hem of her sweatshirt and pulls it over her head. I could tell from the picture she sent earlier that there was no bra beneath her compression shirt from the way her nipples had peaked, just as they are now.

Wordlessly, I wait for her to continue.

She slips out of her shoes, then pushes the waistband of her sweatpants down, leaving her in the shorts that are short enough to sit perfectly in the crease of her thighs. I didn't lie to her the other night—I don't get jealous. But I am possessive. To me, there's a difference. I know only I can make her come as hard as she does, but I am also aware that other men would love to try. Seeing how she arches her back just as she's about to come would be a high for any man.

"Spin."

Lifting on her toes, Fallon spins in a slow circle. Her shorts have ridden up to reveal a couple inches of her ass, and I imagine every person in the class was gifted this view. Fallon isn't cocky. She's very humble and unaware of the effect she has on the people around her, but she's also confident in her body.

It might be one of her sexiest attributes.

Not once has she ever shied away from me.

I've been with women who try to hide themselves every time they're naked. It angers me each time. Not because they're doing it but because they feel they need to. They haven't been with a man who appreciates a woman's body in all its forms. No woman's body is the same, and it's been a treat every time to explore curves I never have before.

But with Fallon? I'd be content exploring only hers. She's wrapped in layers of mystery.

We're short on time. As much as I'd love to drag this out and edge her, there's something I need to show her before we leave. I'll need to make her come quickly again.

The more we fuck, the longer she'll last each time, and the orgasms will only intensify. She probably thinks this is as good as it gets.

My sweet girl.

I slide off the counter and grab her waist, spinning her around and hoisting her up. Her legs wrap around my waist to hold me close, but I need her spread wide open. Her eyes keep darting to the front of the store, undoubtedly watching for people to pass by. I grab her chin and refocus her attention on me. "Eyes on me, Fallon. If you want to come, you won't look anywhere else. Understood?"

"But anyone could see—"

"So?" I rest my hands on her thighs. "It's me and you in here. Who gives a fuck what others think?" I kiss her softly. "Were you happy to see me today?"

"Of course," she whispers, resting her palms against my chest. "I'm always happy to see you, Fitz."

Something warm and sticky oozes through my chest every time she says that. It's so simple. It's something you could say to a stranger. To an acquaintance you haven't seen for a while. But the way Fallon says it to me sounds so honest.

Before I fall down the rabbit hole of why those words feel so heavy, I reiterate what I said to her. "Eyes on me."

"Eyes on you," she repeats, then she kisses me. Her fingers thread through my hair, her tongue slips past my lips, and her chest presses against mine.

The embrace is passionate and raw, and I find myself returning it, almost as if I missed her today. It was as if I felt her absence each time the door opened, and she wasn't the one walking through it. It was as if every time someone passed by her stacks of classic novels, I was brought back to our first encounter. How irritating I found her to be. How degrading she was. How irresistible I found her bright green eyes. How time with her never feels like enough.

Like I'm somehow running out of it quicker than anticipated.

She fumbles for the hem of my shirt but manages to get it up and over my head. Before she can resume our kiss, I remove her shirt and lower to suck her nipple between my lips while kneading her other breast. I don't know if she realizes what she's doing, but she applies pressure to the top of my head to sink lower. She wants my tongue in her cunt.

Happy to oblige, I slip my fingers into her waistband and slide her shorts off. But before I devour, I take a step back and admire. Teasingly, she parts her knees slowly, inch by inch, and scoots closer to the edge of the counter. Even from here, I can see how wet she already is from just a kiss and possibly the anticipation of coming. I want to make this a little more challenging for her. "Do you have any excerpts memorized?"

She blinks. "What?"

I step forward and drag my thumb down her clit. Fuck, I want to taste her. "Something from a book, Fallon."

Her fingertips daintily trace one of the tattoos on my left arm. "Is this your idea of foreplay?"

Placing one hand against her chest, I slowly push her down so she's flat on her back. "Answer."

She squirms when I kiss down her stomach. "Yes, I have the speech from *Pride & Prejudice* memorized."

I drag my nose across her clit. "Recite it."

"Fuck, okay," she murmurs, adjusting her hips. "Um, from the very beginning——"

I suck her clit between my lips.

She sucks in a tight breath. "You cannot be serious right now. Ah, from the first moment, I may almost say…"

I throw my arm across her stomach to stop her wiggling. I'm trying not to laugh at her reactions. This might've been cruel, but I can guarantee she won't ever look at Mr. Darcy the same way again. "Keep going," I encourage when she silences.

She clears her throat. "Of my acquaintance with you…" She moans when I slip my tongue inside her. "I can't—"

I replace my tongue with two of my fingers, curling them inside her and grinning when a shiver rocks her entire body. "You taste so sweet, my little tragedy. You were going to shower and deny me this."

"I'm sorry?" She phrases the apology like a question.

I flick my tongue against her clit repeatedly while moving my fingers steadily inside her. I could come from only this. I wouldn't even need to jerk off. I've had my fair share of pussy, but I can't remember one ever tasting this good. It would be my luck that a woman as bullheaded as her would have the best-tasting pussy. Not only do women like this stress you out, but they get you addicted to the way they taste.

They leave you wanting more.

And that's all I've wanted from her every time we're together. More attitude, more arguments, more pussy. She's like a siren, beckoning me closer and striking my ego down.

It's maddening and alluring all at once.

She cries my name when her back arches off the counter, her fingers pressing into my arm splayed across her stomach. I could stay here and do it all again, but we only have moments before Thomas starts calling.

Raising and grabbing her hips, I slide her off the counter and spin her around so her stomach is pressed against the edge. I realize she's most likely dizzy and disoriented, but my desperation to be inside her is blurring my vision.

I discard my pants in seconds, fist my cock, and slam into her. Gasping from the force, she bends forward, pressing her chest against the counter and gripping the edge. But she doesn't ask me to stop. She doesn't ask to breathe. Instead, she pushes her ass against me and silently encourages me for more. I give it willingly, thrusting unsteadily until I'm able to slow my heart rate a tick.

"Fallon," I rasp, pressing my thumb against her spine. "Fuck, I've thought about this all day." My other hand kneads her ass. "Fuck, fuck," I say repeatedly.

Her breathless moans fill the room. One of the iPads falls off the counter from the rocking, but she doesn't seem to notice or care. I'll buy her a hundred more if she always lets me fuck her like this—raw and submissive.

"Spread your legs a little more, baby."

She scoots her legs apart a couple more inches, allowing me a slightly better angle to drive into her. And that's exactly what does it for her. "Fitz." Her voice scratches. "Right there, right there, right there—"

I cry her name when I come, gifting her two more thrusts before she unravels around me again. I collapse on top of her, our chests moving in tandem as we try to catch our breath. With my eyes closed, my cock twitches inside her as visions of only her fill my mind. I'm tempted to persuade her to stay in tonight, but I must remain wrapped up in her world. Isolating her for my own twisted needs might drive her away. I need to keep living as someone who could be her boyfriend, as a man able to commit.

I press my lips against her shoulder. I won't allow myself to feel guilty. Not about this. *She's the enemy*, I repeat silently to myself. But as often as I say it, I can't make it sound convincing enough. She's an actual threat to my livelihood—to the life I've become used to. She could throw a wrench in FFJ expanding into this area.

Why does that sound obsolete whenever I repeatedly rehearse this same speech in my head?

Fallon's phone buzzes from wherever it landed on the

floor. We haven't even begun closing the store. "I need to show you something." I slowly pull out of her and wait until she's steady on her feet before grabbing her hand. "There was another reason Thomas wanted you out of the store today."

I lead her to the back wall of the store, one of the very few that doesn't have a bookshelf against it. A felt board is hanging on the wall, which I hung today. And pinned against it are two Polaroid pictures. The first is of me and Thomas together, smiling at the camera. The second is a candid Thomas snapped of me hanging the board up. In the photo, I'm glancing over my shoulder with a scowl, and he promised she'd love it when she saw it.

"You'll keep the cameras at the register, but customers can have their pictures taken, or you can offer to take one to add to your board." I kiss the top of her head. "Thomas wanted you to have tangible evidence of the difference you make."

Her silence worries me. I grab her waist and gently turn her around to face me, only to see that her eyes are lined with tears. "Hey," I whisper, "if you don't like it—"

"I love it," she murmurs, sniffling. "I love how much he loves me. And I love that you helped." She slides her arms around my waist and pierces me with her gaze. "Thank you."

I remove myself from her, only to return to the counter and retrieve a camera. With a grin, I beckon her over and lift her to sit on the counter again, standing behind her. "We won't put this on the wall," I say through a laugh, then hold the camera in front of us and press the button.

The camera clicks and pops as it prints the picture. Fallon takes it and fans it, holding it out for me to see. My chest threatens to crack open when it develops.

I don't even recognize the smile on my face.

*hayes*

The return to Boston for the day was planned. It didn't ease the tightness in my stomach or the anticipation of seeing my father, but nothing ever does. I could be coming to him with nothing but good news, but he'd still find something wrong. But I'm hoping he'll be impressed with how quickly I've gathered intel on Fallon and how she's doing so well after only a year.

I didn't tell her where I'd be today. After dinner last night with Thomas and Ansel, we returned to her place and fucked for most of the night, but I didn't stay. Fucking is intimate, but staying overnight places us in a different category. As calming as holding her against my chest is, I can't allow it to get further than that. Waking up next to her with the sun painting her skin and her skin against mine? That's a recipe for disaster.

I wait in my father's office, staring out the office window. Our headquarters are on the top floor of a Boston skyscraper. We've been here as long as I can remember. In fact, we've been here for so long that the building owner allows my father to vote on new tenants. If he doesn't like them, the owner declines their application. My father doesn't have a checklist he uses to decide who gets to set foot in this building; he's just a dick and enjoys having the power to choose.

From our ivory tower, Boston looks small. I can see most of the city from here. Before I became a disappointment to him, one of my favorite things to do as a child was to sit here and count the cars below. The people below look smaller than ants, making me feel big. And it's easy to become arrogant when you're treated like royalty because of the money your family has. Not only did I feel big, but everyone treated me like it—all because of my name. I had no qualifications other than being the son of a big-time CEO.

I've built nothing. I might be considered smart by educational standards, but that's only because I had access to schooling that most children don't. And then there are people like Fallon who have worked for all they have. I envy people like her. She gets to be proud of what she's created. Meanwhile, I carry shame for not accomplishing anything and having everything I could ever want at my fingertips.

And here I stand, willing to tear everything she has apart to impress my father and finally prove myself to him. To possibly earn myself an office here—to earn a place. I might be his son, but he's done a damn good job of making me feel like an outsider my entire life. Even when I graduated with honors, he couldn't find the time to attend my graduation because it wasn't anything compared to what he'd done in his life. That's what he told me, at least.

The door to his office opens and closes, but I don't turn. I recognize the sound of him twisting the lid of his decanter and pouring his expensive whiskey. I know him well enough to know that he's drinking the first glass before pouring himself another—probably to wash the taste of his secretary's pussy out of his mouth before addressing me.

My father has never been known for his looks. He's thin and frail, even though he's only in his fifties, and has a bald spot on the back of his head that shines in the light. He seduced my mother when they were teenagers by bringing flowers from her yard to her each time he mowed it. Her father believed in my father's idea of planting family-friendly retailers in the Boston area and invested.

My mother was the homecoming queen. Even if she hadn't invested thousands in maintaining her youth through procedures, she'd still be considered beautiful. But even with her on his arm, my father grew bored, and even a son couldn't fill the void. Money seemed to satisfy him until the affairs started. He seems to keep grasping for something that he can't find.

All he's accomplished is ensuring his family hates him.

He appears next to me and searches the skyline. He doesn't greet me. He doesn't pat me on the back. He doesn't even offer me a drink. All he says is, "What have you learned from your time in Sanderling, Hayes?"

"Fallon has built relationships with publishers and agents," I begin, sliding my hands into my pockets. "She stocks books written by indie authors. She attends book conventions every year to maintain relationships. She's personable. Authors are drawn to her because she doesn't view them as means to an end."

I shove the gnawing feeling in my chest down. Why does the idea of betraying her make me so nauseous?

"Because of that, she receives special treatment from agents." A muscle in my jaw feathers when I recall her dinner with Ryan. "She connects with local businesses in Sanderling and partners with them to draw in new customers."

He finishes his second glass and silently waits for more.

"She has multiple shipments of inventory a week. That's how quickly she's growing. It makes sense that she'd want to expand into a new location this quickly." I can't help the smile that accompanies the following thought. "She's brilliant."

"That may be so," my father grunts, "but she's young and sounds too trusting. Naive. She won't last in the business world. We need to obliterate her before she fails on her own."

She could last if I helped her. She's done well on her own, but I have access to thousands more resources for her. Fallon would never agree to be under our umbrella. She knows what she's built is far too valuable for that. She values relationships. She'll see right through us.

"Return to Sanderling," he demands. "Find out more about her expansion plans. What her dreams are." He slaps me on the back. "We need to know what we're crushing."

He leaves me standing alone.

I look down at the people crossing the street below, focusing on a mother pushing a stroller. That child is loved. They'll most likely be encouraged. Adored. And I no longer feel big compared to them. Ironically, I've never felt smaller.

---

I return to Sanderling late. I was stuck in Boston traffic. Even weaving in and out on my bike only halves travel time. I haven't spoken to Fallon today, nor has she reached out. I've picked up on her anxious habits, and I'm sure it's driven her crazy not hearing from me today. Thomas probably encouraged her not to text me. Even though he's with Ansel, it's apparent after talking to him that he has been on the dating scene for a while. He knows all the tricks.

I knock on Fallon's door but hear no movement inside. I check the time on my Apple Watch. She wouldn't be at the store. It closed two hours ago. She could be at dinner with Thomas, but that'd still be later than usual.

I hop on my bike and ride over to her Pilates studio, pleased to see her through the window. She's chatting with another woman, but her recent joyous smile is missing. She's engaged in the conversation, but she's jittery.

She missed me.

I don't know what I'm doing here. I should go home. We've seen each other every day for a couple weeks now. She's getting attached to me. Continuing to give her false hope about what we are seems cruel, but I can't make myself move. I'm content to just watch her.

She slips her sweatshirt on. She's wearing a pair of leggings today that I've yet to see her in, and I wonder if it's a pair she picked up yesterday. They're skintight and a light blue, leaving little to the imagination when she bends over to retrieve her bag and check her phone, frowning.

I can't help but grin. A sense of power is bestowed upon someone when you wait anxiously for their text, and she's given that to me. Now I know she wants to hear from me. That's something to keep in my back pocket.

I sit on my bike and cross my arms when she walks out of the studio with much less pep in her step than usual. But when she looks across the lot and notices me, a visible sense of relief washes over her, and the tension in her shoulders eases.

Fuck, I'm an asshole.

I let her come to me, though I'm tempted to cross the lot and scoop her into my arms. She's become a welcome bad habit these last few days. Her presence centers me. Getting lost in her distracts me from what I have to do to her.

She drops her phone into her bag and crosses her arms

upon approach. A chuckle rumbles deep in my chest from the stubborn way she purses her lips. She's clearly annoyed that I didn't talk to her at all today, and I'm interested to find out if she'll say anything about it or fall for my charm again.

"Miss me?" I ask as she nears.

She shrugs a shoulder but doesn't say a word. She isn't afraid of me—I'll give her that. She isn't looking away. I have never been with anyone as challenging as her.

"You can't expect me to trust you if you're going to disappear," she says after a moment. Her voice didn't even shake.

"I didn't disappear." I grab the pocket of her hoodie and drag her closer. "I went to Boston for the day."

She quirks an eyebrow. "I didn't realize they don't have cell service there. My apologies."

I bite back a laugh. "Write them a strongly-worded letter."

She shoves my hand away. "I'm being serious, Fitz. I don't know what this is." She motions between her body and mine. "But I'm not just… something to do. You can't just show up and expect to come to my apartment after ignoring me."

I cock my head. "Who said I wanted to come over?"

She is quick to call me on my bullshit. "You do. You wouldn't be here otherwise. You don't strike me as the type of guy who'd just come here because you want to say hi."

Oddly, hearing that feels like a punch in the gut. "Fallon, do you think I'm just lingering around to fuck you?"

She throws her arms up. "I don't know!"

I stand, my brow furrowed as I cup her chin in my hand and tilt her head back. Unable to stand the distance, I lean in and kiss her softly. "Hi," I murmur against her lips.

She tries to fight it. She gives a very valiant effort for a full minute. She waits long enough to make me question if I did take it a step too far by not texting her today. But then, she wraps her arms around my waist and buries her head against my chest. "You drive me mad," she whispers.

I kiss the top of her head. "Is that a bad thing?"

"I don't know what to expect from this." The honesty behind those green eyes of hers punctures my chest. "I'm not the type of girl to just… mess around, Fitz. I'm not saying you need to be my boyfriend, but if you're going to fuck me daily, I deserve the respect of communication."

"You're right, Fallon." And she is. I might be a dick, but she doesn't deserve to be disregarded when she's given so much of herself to me already. "I'm sorry."

"Thank you." She lifts to her toes and puts effort into our next kiss. "Do you really not want to come over?"

Of course, I want to come over. I want to fuck you until you're asleep on my chest. But instead, I say, "Only if you'd like for me to come over. I just wanted to see you."

"Oh yeah?" Her mouth curves into a playful grin. "What if I want to play board games all night?"

I can't resist scowling. "Naked board games?"

She rolls her eyes. "Oh, brother."

*fallon*

We did not play board games last night. I tried. Jokingly, of course. When we arrived at my apartment, I pulled Monopoly out and placed it on the table. Fitz ended up knocking it off the table and laying me down on it instead, nearly breaking one of the legs from how hard he fucked me. I might be delusional, but the time apart seemed to be as difficult for him as it was for me. I did a great job of convincing myself yesterday that I'd most likely never hear from him again and that he'd already grown bored.

But he's been at the store with me all day today and sends me hourly texts to be a passive-aggressive asshole, but at least he's taking what I said seriously. His most recent text was a picture of Thomas eating a brownie in the storeroom and flipping off the camera. Their blossoming friendship is adorable, but I'd never tell them that.

A minute before closing, I hear someone walk through the door. Usually, I wouldn't mind staying open for them to peruse, but Fitz promised a surprise this evening. But when I look toward the front, I'm pleasantly surprised to see Andrew. He seems to be the lesser of two evils when it comes to Fitz's friends. "Andrew!" I greet. "What are you doing here?"

Andrew waves lazily. "Fitz needs to borrow my car for the evening. I'm here to pick up his bike and take it back to his place." He looks around the store. "Where is the bastard?"

I hook my thumb over my shoulder. "Doing his job in the storeroom, hopefully. Why does he need your car?"

Andrew shrugs, but his face gives it away. He knows the reason but was probably told not to spoil the surprise.

I wrinkle my nose. "I'm surprised you ride."

"Fuck," he mutters, leaning against the counter. "I don't. I hate that Fitz does. But he taught me how when we were teenagers. I remember enough to make it back to his place."

I still find it a little strange that Fitz hasn't invited me over yet. "Ah, yeah. Where does he live again? He told me which building, but I forgot." I'm lying, of course. Fitz hasn't given me any indication of where he lives.

"Pleasant Park," he replies.

*Pleasant Park?* He has to be mistaken. That building has condos that rent for thousands a month. I'm not paying Fitz enough to live there. I know he mentioned his dad owning a business once but *goddamn*. Why is he working for me if he can afford to live there?

I nod absentmindedly. "Right. I haven't been there yet."

It takes seconds for Andrew to notice my confusion, but he doesn't try to explain further. Instead, he clears his throat and points toward the backroom. "I'll just, uh, go grab Fitz's keys from him and be on my way."

I drum my fingers against the countertop, not bothering to say goodbye to Andrew. Okay, so there's something Fitz isn't telling me. Why did he need a job here while living in a place like Pleasant Park? Why did he actually leave Boston? If I had spidey senses, they'd be tingling.

Fitz and Andrew emerge together from the back. If Andrew warned him about spilling his secret, Fitz shows no sign of it. He tells Andrew goodbye before kissing me. "Ready?"

"Mhm," I hum, then shout to Thomas that we're leaving and to lock the door behind us. "Let's go."

---

We don't exchange pleasantries, nor does Fitz tell me where we're going or what our plans are for this evening. And honestly, I don't think I should ask. My mind is swirling with so many questions and scenarios that I don't even hear him ask me a question until he puts his hand on my leg.

"Are you okay?" he repeats.

I blink to clear the fog. "Um, yeah. Why?"

It's evident from his expression that he doesn't believe me. "You haven't said a word since we left."

"I'd love to see your place," I blurt out.

He doesn't flinch or shy away. Instead, he shakes his head with a grin. "I wondered how long it'd take you." He makes a dramatic show of looking at his watch. "Ten minutes."

I mutter an obscenity under my breath. He was baiting me the entire time, just waiting for me to pry.

"Trust fund? Nepo baby?" I twist the ends of my hair. "I toured one of those condos with Thomas once just for the hell of it. Living in one is in my five-year plan."

He listens silently.

"I'm one year into my five-year plan," I continue. "Even then, I don't know if I'll be able to afford it—"

"You will," he assures. "At the rate you're going? It won't even be five years. Two years, maybe."

"Great." There's a hint of sarcasm in my tone. "But you're two weeks into working at the store, and you have one."

He releases a deep sigh.

"Were you just never going to invite me over?"

"I hadn't given it much thought," he mumbles.

"Okay." I pull my leg away from his hand. "Got it."

"Fallon," he sighs. "It's not because I don't want to invite you over. Do you want to come over? We can go right now."

I narrow my eyes at him. "*No.*"

He pulls into the lot across from the lighthouse and switches the car off. The tension between us is thick and filled with frustration. I'm realizing just how little I know about the man I've let explore my entire body these last two weeks.

"I have something planned for us," he says after a moment. "And I'd still like to show you."

"You're avoiding being honest with me, Fitz."

He taps his fingers against the steering wheel and stares at the water crashing onto the rocks surrounding the lighthouse, quiet for a long moment. "I'm trying to find out who I am outside my family's expectations. That's why I'm here." His jaw clenches and releases. "Do I have money? Yes. But that shouldn't change your opinion about me."

"It doesn't," I say quickly. "Fitz, I don't care where you live or if you have money. I just feel like there are things you're not sharing with me. Why wouldn't you invite me over?"

"Because I like being where you're most comfortable."

I nod slowly while trying to read between the lines of everything he's saying. "Are you not comfortable at your place? Are you afraid I won't be?"

He swipes a hand down his face. My line of questioning is agitating him. This isn't the first time he's avoided having an honest conversation with me. But I need to be able to compromise with him. He's already shared more than he wanted.

"Okay," I whisper, placing my hand over his. "Thank you for telling me. Show me what you have planned for us."

With a steadying breath, he nods and exits the car, coming to my side to open the door for me. Each time he does that, it reminds me of my father, which only makes my fondness for him grow. I watch him go to the trunk with a smile on my face, clapping my hand over my mouth when he retrieves a rather large picnic basket. Now I understand why he didn't want to carry both me and the basket on his bike.

"Fitz!" I exclaim, bouncing on my toes.

He finally relaxes into a smile and takes my hand, tugging me with him up the steps of the lighthouse until we're at the top. The setting sun casts a warm glow through the small window, providing us with just enough light to dine comfortably. Fitz sets the basket down and flips the lid open, pulling out a blanket to spread across the floor.

I lower to my knees, anxiously awaiting to see what he brought. "Did Andrew put the basket together?"

"Fuck no," he says with a laugh. "It was catered."

I don't know of any places that cater picnic baskets here, which means Andrew picked it up in Boston.

Fitz spreads a variety of foods across the blanket. It's way more than either of us will eat. Shredded chicken, various sauces, grilled asparagus, ripe tomatoes, hummus, potato salad, foods I don't even recognize, and a bottle of wine.

He dispenses the utensils and napkins, puts a little of

everything on a plate for me, and then fills my wine glass. I'm overcome with gratitude at this grand gesture, leaning forward to throw my arms around his neck and kissing him. He nearly drops my plate but sets it down in front of me before fully engaging in the embrace, pulling me into his lap to deepen the kiss.

"This is amazing," I murmur against his lips, kissing him twice more. "Truly, Fitz. Thank you for arranging this."

He gazes into my eyes. "You're happy?"

I place my palm against his cheek. "So very happy."

He kisses the corner of my mouth before readjusting me in his lap. "You're the dessert, so eat."

I relax against his chest with a sated smile. I doubt I'll be able to stop smiling for days to come. "If only you brought grapes to feed me." I pop a piece of chicken into my mouth.

He hands me the wine glass. "Next time."

We spend an hour eating, talking, and drinking the entire bottle of wine. We discussed my upcoming trip to California—a trip he still wants to partake in. "After California, there's a banquet for small businesses." I finish my third glass of wine. I need to slow down. "Would you like to be my date?"

He kisses my neck. "Of course."

It could be from the wine, but my entire body warms at his confirmation. That's two weeks away, but him agreeing to be my date makes it seem like we'll still be doing this by then.

"I'm attending a baby shower in California." I don't know why sharing that tidbit of information felt important. "I hope you can keep yourself entertained."

He sucks my earlobe between his lips.

"I was the first one to learn about her pregnancy," I continue. "It's a superpower I have."

That gets his attention enough for him to sit up. "What?"

I draw shapes on his knee. "Mm, my superpower. I can always tell when a woman is pregnant." I trace a heart. "They emit a glow. I've always been able to tell."

"Maybe we should have you studied." He lays down on his back and pulls me with him, stroking my back. "This banquet of yours... you said it's only for small businesses?"

"Mm," I hum, balancing my chin atop my hand on his chest. "It's our second year attending. With any luck, I'll be attending next year's events with two locations."

His hand stills. "Oh?"

Frowning, I shrug slightly. "I applied for a location in the city. Something is holding it up. I don't think there's a reason it wouldn't be approved, but they won't give me any information on what could be taking so long. My approval to open Shoreline Scribes last year was approved almost instantly."

"Maybe there's a competing offer," he offers.

I've considered that possibility along with many others. "Maybe, but I'm putting all my assets into this possible second location. I've already taken out a loan."

Genuine concern fills his face. "Fallon, why?"

"Because I have big dreams." I'm positive my words are starting to slur. "I'm able to make the payments from Shoreline's revenue. I don't want a chain of stores. This next location will have more than just books. I've talked with the owner of Corner Brews, and she's willing to share the space. It'll be a joint venture. She'll pay me to rent the space and keep everything she earns from sales."

"Have you had contracts drawn up?"

"God." I roll my eyes with a deep sigh. "Yes. And that was another unexpected expense. Lawyers aren't cheap."

"The good ones never are," he mutters.

I wonder how he knows that, but I decide not to press him for any more information tonight, not when he's gone to all this trouble to convince me he's not using me just for sex.

Instead, I scoot closer to him until I'm practically lying on his chest—a position he seems to favor. "Fitz," I whisper, tracing his jawline. "I think I'm starting to like you."

He closes his arms around me, then studies me for a quiet moment. Something unreadable behind his eyes makes me wary, and I regret saying it aloud for a moment.

But then, he leans up and kisses me. "Likewise."

And my universe recenters.

*hayes*

I could kill Andrew. I still might. I could stash Fallon on the balcony, lock the door, and knock him over the head with a beer bottle. It's not that I didn't want to invite Fallon over eventually; it's that I didn't have an excuse yet for how I could afford a condo in one of the most prestigious buildings in Sanderling. I didn't know how long I'd be here, so I signed a month-to-month lease. As I continue to quickly gather the information I need on Fallon, I could be out as early as next month. But I can't continue holding out on her now that she knows. She would grow more suspicious.

She sways down the hallway, dragging her fingertips along the wall as she hums a song I'm positive she's making up. She had as much wine as I did, but she's much smaller than me, and I don't think she drinks often. After one glass, I should've stopped her, but her relaxed smile was radiant.

When she goes a little too far down the hall, I retrieve her by hooking my finger in her waistband and dragging her back, using my other hand to unlock the door to my condo. Andrew is sitting at the bar, working on his laptop and drinking a beer. He doesn't seem surprised to see Fallon but does toss me an apologetic grin. Out of both my idiotic friends, I thought Jace would be the one to slip.

"Andrew," I greet dryly.

"Andrew," Fallon repeats in a mocking deep tone. "God, he's so personable, isn't he? Hi, Andrew."

Andrew grins, amused.

"Fallon is drunk," I mutter, still holding onto her pants so she doesn't topple over or wander off.

"Aw, pookie." She presses on the tip of my nose with her index finger. "Don't be so grumpy. Show me around."

I blink. No one has ever done that to me, nor would I allow it from anyone else, but she's looking at me with round eyes and a pouty bottom lip, and I swear something inside my chest thumps. I don't have a heart, so it must be the early signs of a stroke. "You said you toured this building."

"I did." She rolls her eyes. "But you weren't here yet. I want to see how you decorated, if you're clean, and if any dead bodies are stashed away somewhere… the basics."

Andrew regards her warmly.

Fuck, he sees it, too. I haven't just imagined it. I'm not under a spell. She really is magnetic to be around.

"I'll show you the guest room," Andrew offers, shutting his laptop and standing. "Fitz will get you some water."

He's allowing me a moment to catch my breath because that's what he's used to doing when I have a woman over. When we were roommates during college, Andrew would keep them entertained while I stepped outside to just relax. Emotions and expectations tend to overwhelm me. But oddly enough, I don't find myself craving space from Fallon.

I don't deny his offer, though. She does need water.

Fallon practically skips over to Andrew and laces her arm through his, allowing him to lead her across the flat into the guest room. I listen to her sounds of awe at the decor from where I remain in the kitchen while filling her glass with sparkling water. Her place is nicely decorated, but it's attuned to her taste. I've never been able to customize any place I've lived. I wouldn't even know where to start or what I like. Every room I've had, every house we've lived in, every place we've stayed has been carefully planned. We had a reputation to maintain.

The son of a CEO billionaire with a Spiderman bedroom just wouldn't fit the aesthetic my mother always wanted to achieve. Instead, I had fucking sailboats and neutral colors. I don't even like sailing that much. We own a yacht, but I always hire someone to take us out on the water, even after my years of lessons on how to be seaworthy.

Fallon reappears next to me, shoeless.

"You've made yourself at home." I hand her the glass. "Drink up, *pookie*. I want you sober before I take you home."

She scrunches her nose before taking a sip. "Fitz," she whispers, casting a quick glance over her shoulder at Andrew before returning to me. "I want to see *your* bedroom."

Chuckling, I tuck a strand of hair behind her ear. "Oh yeah? And why's that, Fallon?"

She hides her smile behind the glass. "It's a secret."

My little beast is hungry.

I glance over at Andrew, gauging his reaction to my silent question. He responds with a shrug. That's his way of telling me he'll leave the decision to me.

I lean against the counter and fold my arms over my chest. "We don't have secrets. Andrew and I have shared many things, including women. We'd like to share you tonight."

She chokes on her water. That might've sobered her up a little. "I'm sorry, what? Share me?"

I remove the glass from her hands and place it on the counter, then wrap my arm around her waist and pull her flush against me. "Share you," I repeat, brushing my lips against hers. "Does that interest you?"

She swallows thickly and holds herself tightly against me, either out of fear or needing to feel safe. We won't force her into it, but I believe she'd enjoy herself with both of us.

But when I look into her eyes, I don't see fear. The slight wrinkle between her eyebrows mirrors disappointment. "You… you'd be okay with someone else touching me?"

She's reaching for something deeper than I'm capable of giving her. I'm possessive over the women I'm sleeping with, but I'm also okay sharing them for experiences such as these. Andrew is my most trusted friend. Like me, he doesn't allow feelings to get involved with the women he's with.

This will be the only time he touches Fallon unless it's something she asks for from me again. It would only become a problem if she preferred him over me, which she wouldn't.

"Yes." I pull down on her bottom lip with my thumb. "As long as it's something we both want. Don't overthink it." I kiss her again, longer this time. "Don't label it. Don't assign an expectation to it. Just let us take care of you."

"I, um…" Her cheeks turn pink. "I've never had a threesome," she confesses, as if that's new information.

"We love popping cherries." I spin her around and lift her onto the counter. "Anything you don't want to do, we won't."

She looks at Andrew over my shoulder while gnawing

on her bottom lip. I know she finds him attractive. Like me, women never turn him down. Admittedly, she's fighting this harder than we're used to. Most, if not all, women we approach with the offer jump at the opportunity.

It's done amazing things for our egos.

A sudden protective instinct befalls me. I return her attention to me by moving so she can't see Andrew behind me. "Hey, we don't have to do this. If you're uncomfortable, say the word. It can be just us tonight."

"I don't want to disappoint you," she whispers.

I need to rectify this immediately. Wrapping her legs around my waist, I balance an arm beneath her and carry her into my room, closing the door behind us. Andrew won't even allow himself to be disappointed about losing out on tasting her. That's one of the best qualities about him. Like me, he doesn't feel anything.

I place her on the edge of my bed and lower to my knees before her, balancing my hands on her thighs. Her eyes are lowered, and it's the first time she hasn't held firm with me.

"Baby, look at me," I urge her gently.

She does the opposite, of course. Instead of looking at me, she tips her head all the way back and stares at the ceiling. "I'm just so inexperienced, Fitz. And it's not even just that."

I squeeze her thighs. "What is it?"

She laughs, but it's not because she finds this situation funny. It sounds more akin to being annoyed with herself. "Because I'm a romantic." She lowers her head and shrugs. "I read too many books, maybe. If I'm with someone, I only want to be with them. I know sex is just sex, but it's never been that way with me. It always meant something."

I nod slowly, trying to understand. To me, sex has

always been exactly that. Just sex. I've never allowed it to be more than that with anyone. "Are you afraid you'll develop feelings for Andrew?"

"No." This time, she does hold my gaze. She stares straight into my eyes and doesn't waver when she says, "I only want to sleep with you. I only want you."

I have… never heard those words.

I don't know what to do with the feelings that accompany her confession. My habit of shoving them down and burying them doesn't seem to work when she's near me. Instead, I always feel everything simultaneously, making me want to bolt. She's piercing pieces of me that no one ever has.

I should ask her to leave. She's getting too close. I'm losing myself in her more and more each day. But I don't ask her to go. I don't shove her away. I do something far worse.

I say, "Stay with me tonight."

---

I dropped Fallon off at the store early this morning. She fell asleep on my chest last night and remained there until my alarm woke her up this morning. Like I anticipated, seeing her first thing in the morning was a terrible idea. Her hair was a mess, one of her cheeks was red from where she laid on me all night, and she smelled of sex and my detergent.

She was divine.

And the morning shower sex we had was even better. It was the first time she went down on me, and now all I can think of while driving to Boston is how she looked with her mouth wrapped around my cock. The sounds she made when she gagged from how deep I was in her throat. The tears that fell from her eyes when she looked up at me as I came.

Fuck, I'm hard again. I can't walk into the meeting with my father like this.

I take the elevator to the top floor, ignore the secretary at the front, and find one of the empty offices and close the door. I take a seat the desk and scoot forward. If anyone walks in, they won't immediately see me jerking off.

I unzip my pants and take my cock out, fisting it and pumping quickly. I'm throbbing from only the thought of her, whispering her name when I recall the way I had her bent over the bed last night. "Fuck," I whisper, my eyes falling closed when I think of how raspy her moans are when she comes for me. I swell in my fist, my balls tightening as visions of her flash continuously through my mind.

"Fallon," I groan, imagining its her hand wrapped around me instead. "Fallon," I say again. "Fuck, fuck…" My cock jerks in my hand as I come, coating my stomach as I pant.

I blink as I'm brought back to reality. I have never needed to jerk off just to get someone off my mind. I'm a risky motherfucker but I stare at the door with the realization that I didn't even bother locking it. I just wanted to imagine her.

I tuck my cock back into my pants and grab tissues from the box sitting atop the desk to clean myself.

What the fuck is she doing to me?

I pull my phone from my pocket and shoot her a text.

**Made it to Boston.**

'Jerked off in the office while thinking of you' is what I'm tempted to say next, but I refrain.

Say hi to the Red Sox for me.

I could take her on a date to Fenway Park this summer. We're season ticket holders. I'm getting way ahead of myself. I doubt she'll ever speak to me again once she finds out what I've done—what I'm about to do.

With a sigh, I slip my phone back into my pocket without replying to her text.

*hayes*

I walk into my father's office, resolved to find a way out of this without hurting Fallon. There has to be a middle ground we can reach that doesn't involve trying to crush her. Ideally, I want to buy myself more time with her. I could lie to him and tell him I haven't found anything yet. Our last meeting was only two days ago. I don't understand why he's already requested another meeting with me. I know it's not because he had high expectations of following through with my task this quickly.

He's on the phone, so I sit in the chair across from his desk. As a child, he was my hero. I'd listen to his phone calls, then pretend to be on a call with the old cellphone he gave me to carry around. I'd pretend not to hear him fighting with my mother when she'd bring me to the office. It was the only time I spent with him. His evenings were always full. As an adult, I remember spending more time with the nanny than either of my parents. My mother would go through phases of loving me dearly and then hating me entirely.

I don't know if I reminded her of him, but that's one of the reasons I grew to despise him. Not only did the way he treated my mother hurt their marriage, but his actions directly impacted how she treated me. There would be days she couldn't get out of bed. I would try to lie down with her and watch a movie, but she'd send me away so she could sleep.

My father puts the receiver down and leans back in his chair, pressing a button and calling for his secretary to come in. Less than a minute later, the door opens, and I hear the grating voice of his eighth secretary. They keep getting younger. I believe this one is in her thirties and is most likely hoping that she'll be the one to get Frank to leave his wife.

He never will. As rich as he is, he won't give my mother the satisfaction of paying alimony, and admitting defeat would be too big of a hit to his ego. He's content to continue fucking his secretaries until he grows bored of them and hires a new one. Cynthia, his current secretary, could pass for a younger version of my mother, which adds another layer to this twisted dynamic.

"Bring me a glass of whiskey," Frank grunts.

"Right away," she says, sashaying to the drink cart and pouring him a glass. "Would you like a glass, Hayes?"

"No," I reply dryly, refusing to look at her.

Frank looks at her with disinterest. She doesn't even realize her days are numbered. His next victim will probably be younger than me, just to prove to himself that he can still fuck someone that young. What he refuses to accept is that women only sleep with him because of his money. He sends them on expensive vacations every year and spoils them with jewelry in exchange for their silence. They all sign NDAs, but he likes to sweeten the deal. He believes women can't be trusted.

Cynthia leans forward when she delivers his drink to him, giving him a view of her ample cleavage. He takes the bait, lustfully staring at her until she closes the door of his office behind her. I know exactly what he'll be doing when I leave today. Cynthia.

Anxious to return to Sanderling, I ask, "Why am I here?"

He finishes his whiskey in one swallow and sets the glass down. "Raquel is pregnant. She doesn't know who the father is. I know it's not you."

"Could be Jace," I mutter, unsurprised by this tidbit of information but wondering why the fuck it required me to come to Boston. "She has a roster of men."

"She's always been a beautiful girl." He sighs deeply. "When her father became my partner, it was always expected that the two of you would marry someday."

I've heard all this before. Being with Raquel was always one of the many expectations placed on me. As a teenager, I considered it. She lost her virginity to me in the pool-house one summer, but neither of us wanted to commit. We were way too bored and had access to way too much money. It wasn't until recently that she started pressuring me to settle and choose her to do it with, but my feelings hadn't changed.

Her decision to sleep with Jace cemented that I could never be with her. She did it to get a reaction from me. I wouldn't ever be able to trust a woman who uses manipulation like that. "What does any of this have to do with me?"

"She's afraid to tell her father," he continues, standing to refill his glass. I'd wager it's his tenth glass of whiskey today. "She came to me yesterday and asked what she should do. She doesn't want to get rid of it. I suggested that."

"Of course you did." I wouldn't be surprised if he encouraged my mother to do the same when she was pregnant with me. "Again, what the fuck does this have to do with me?"

Raquel's father still owns half the company. He and my father golf together every Sunday. I don't understand why he can't just tell her father or why it required me to drive here and hear about Raquel's fatherless child.

He returns to his desk. "You and Raquel will announce your engagement in the paper. After that, she'll inform her father of the pregnancy. He'll assume it's your child."

I'm rendered utterly speechless.

He just hit me with a shit ton of bricks.

"You'll be assigned an official position in the company." He's trying to soften the blow. "You'll be given shares, and your vote will count for twenty-five percent in all business matters."

"For this fucking child that isn't even mine?" I stand, but I have nowhere to go. I can't seem to unclench my fists. "This is a joke, right? You're not seriously shackling me to Raquel and trying to buy me off with shares that I'm already going to inherit anyway? I won't agree to this."

I want to call my mother for the first time in a long time. She's most likely at a spa in the fucking rainforest, but she won't allow him to go through with this. There has to be some motherly instinct left in her to protect me from this.

Frank remains eerily calm. "You will marry her, Hayes. I hold your entire future in the palm of my hand. You've always believed you're entitled to this company, but you forget I can take it all away from you instantly."

My chest heaves. "I'm your *son*."

"And as my son, you will uphold any responsibility I give you if you want to sustain the life you've been given." His fist thumps against his desk. "You are going to do this, Hayes."

I do not want a future in the company like this. It's not worth my freedom being stripped away to appease

Raquel's father. "Why do you even care what her father thinks?"

"He is the majority shareholder!" Frank barks. "He owns fifty-one percent of this company. And you know as well as I do that he's always expected you and Raquel together. She hasn't informed him that the two of you are no longer together. He'll believe the child is yours. If you don't do this, he'll assume you left her after learning about the child. And that's what Raquel threatened during our meeting."

"Fuck!" I shout. Her father could buy mine out or pressure the board to relieve him of his seat. Not only would my future be at risk, but everything my mother is used to could be stripped away. We'd have enough money to sustain us our entire lives, but everything my father built would be in someone else's hands. Our entire legacy would be gone.

But that still doesn't mean I want to earn my place in this company by being with someone I can't stand.

My phone buzzes in my pocket. I pull it out to find a text from Fallon. She sent me a selfie of her sticking her tongue out and crossing her eyes, followed by a series of texts.

> Bored. There's a lull.
>
> I kinda miss you.
>
> Can we get sushi tonight?
>
> (Say yes.)

I stare at her picture, mind racing.

"I have different conditions," I whisper, pocketing my phone. "And I want a contract drawn to reflect your agreement. Only then will I agree to your demands."

"You're not in the position—"

"I am," I interrupt before he can spew more bullshit. "Just because you're threatening my future in this company, I can still walk away. I'm not your puppet. I agreed to gather information on Fallon because I believed it would make you respect me. I realize now that you're incapable of that."

Frank narrows his eyes. He wants to call my bluff, but his curiosity will win. "What do you want?"

If I walk away and deny him this request, his vengeance toward Fallon and her success will increase. It's up to me to protect her and her future. "I want you to forget her name. I want you to forget she exists."

"Her," he repeats. "*Her…* the girl from Sanderling? For what reason?"

I calmly return to my chair. He doesn't need reasoning. "You won't pursue her any further, nor will you use any of the company's resources to bury her business. You will withdraw your application to the space in Sanderling immediately."

"And if I refuse?"

"I walk," I reply plainly. "And I help her grow her business. You might believe I haven't paid attention to how FFJ operates, but I've logged enough hours here to learn the ins and outs. I know our resources. I graduated with honors from Boston University—the same one you attended, though if I recall, you did *not* graduate with honors."

He clenches his fist.

"Andrew will follow me," I continue. "Jace's father will assist with any tech we need. You always said it's important to have powerful friends, Frank." My smug grin is most likely making his pulse skyrocket. "I listened. Do we have a deal?"

His nostrils flare with each tight breath. "You're willing to do this for some woman you hardly know? You're risking your entire future on a maybe, Hayes."

"She is more than a maybe." I roll my shoulders back. I have never been more confident about anything in my life. Fallon will achieve everything she's hoped for. "And I will not be the reason she fails. Neither will you."

He doesn't utter a word for a long time. Frank is a dick, but he's a smart businessman. He's dissecting every outcome. Fallon *is* a threat. He was correct in assuming that. But me and Fallon as a team? FFJ would take a direct hit.

I'd make sure of that.

"And not only will you leave her alone, but you'll sponsor the upcoming banquet in Sanderling that supports small businesses." I might as well sweeten the deal while he's weakest. "FFJ will present a check to a small business. Each member of the board will cast a vote to decide who receives it." Fallon would kill me if she learned I forced him to grant Shoreline Scribes the money. It stays fair this way.

He picks up his receiver and presses a button. "Cynthia," he grunts. "Get Jerry on the line. I need a contract drawn up."

*fallon*

usic blares through my apartment as I sing to each song from my Spotify blend. My suitcase is on my bed while I arrange an array of shorts and tank tops in neat piles beside it. I picked up a few new pieces for California when I went thrifting. Swimming in the ocean will still be too cold, but I can't wait to sink into the sand. Fitz has visited California often and promised to take me to all his favorite spots, including the Santa Monica pier.

We leave in a few days. Like last year, Ansel will assist Thomas with running the store while I'm gone. I haven't told Fitz yet, but Thomas encouraged me to add two days to our sightseeing trip and experience more things together. I plan on telling Fitz the news at dinner, which will hopefully be sushi.

I haven't heard much from Fitz today. The last text I received was an hour ago when he left Boston to come here. I can't complain—his minimal texts were still texts. He listened to what I said and accounted for my feelings. Baby steps. I might ask for a FaceTime call next.

I disappear into my closet momentarily to pull a few more clothes, nearly screaming when I return to my bedroom to see him sitting on the bed. I collapse against the bathroom door, clothes at my feet from dropping them, and clutch my chest. The music was so loud that I didn't hear him coming in. I had texted him the code to enter the building and told him I'd keep the door unlocked for him, but fuck.

"Alexa!" I shout. "Stop!"

The music ceases. All that's left is the sound of my heart thumping rapidly in my chest. "Hi," I say, breathless.

He looks… exhausted. His eyes are sunk in, his hair matted to his scalp from wearing his helmet, and his shoulders slumped forward. He looks defeated. I didn't ask why he had to return to Boston after just going there a couple days ago, but whatever it was, it doesn't seem like he enjoyed it.

I approach him like he's a wounded dog and stand between his knees, running my hand through his hair. "Are you okay? What's wrong?"

He rests his forehead against my stomach, his arms encircling my waist. He doesn't respond to my question verbally, but this response is telling.

"Hey." I tug his hair gently. "Talk to me, Fitz."

He releases a weary sigh, then lifts his head to look at me. "Are you hungry? Do you still want sushi?"

Again, he wants to avoid conversing with me, but if something bothers him, I want to be part of it.

I shimmy out of his arms and sit beside him on my bed, knocking his knee with mine. "I want to know what's up."

For a long moment, he doesn't move. I'm not even sure he's breathing. He won't even look at me. But then, he slowly stands and leans against my bedroom door. In an instant, his entire demeanor changes. It's as if he slips a mask on. "This isn't going to work between us, Fallon. I need space."

I blink. My lips part.

That wasn't what I was expecting.

He just ripped the band-aid right off.

"I, um," I stutter, unable to process what he said. To be fair, we never defined what *this* is, but this is a stark contrast to what we were just this morning. "What happened?"

His nonchalant shrug might make me crash out. "Nothing. I just realized it could never work. You're wanting more from me than I'm willing to give."

I stand, immediately defensive. "I haven't asked anything from you, Fitz. I haven't demanded anything." A lump forms in my throat as I fight back tears. "I don't understand. Is this because I stayed over last night?"

He doesn't say anything. He doesn't convey any emotion whatsoever. I'm unable to read him.

I step closer. "Just talk to me, Fitz. Help me understand."

But the look he gives me in return for my plea isn't one I've seen before. It's an unsettling mixture of disappointment and disdain. "Are you going to beg me to stay, Fallon?"

I fall back two steps. "You're being cruel."

"And you're being desperate." He approaches me, chasing me when I place more distance between us. "Never ask a man why he's leaving you, Fallon. You're better than that." He grabs my chin between his fingers and holds me still, not even flinching when a tear slips from my eye. "You don't know me like you think you do. You handed yourself over so easily."

I jerk my chin away. "So, I was just a game to you?"

His replying chuckle cuts me raw. "A game would imply a challenge. You weren't even that."

I turn my head away, unable to stand looking at him. I'm at war with myself. Half of me wants to touch him— to ask him to kiss me. The other half of me, the feminist, logical side of me, never wants to see him again. Do I listen to my heart or my mind?

You should never allow a man to tell you more than once that he doesn't want you. I always hoped that advice would never be relative to me. I prayed I'd never be the girl who needed to be reminded of that, but that's precisely what I've become. Because I *do* want to hear it again. I *do* want to figure out exactly why he's letting me go. I want to know what changed from this morning to this moment. But I can't chase the snake and ask why he bit me.

I can't tell him all the reasons I don't deserve this.

Instead of demanding reasons, I whisper, "Get out."

He doesn't move. The heat of his gaze is overwhelming. I can't breathe. Even as he breaks my heart, I long for him to tell me he's joking—that this was some sick joke he hopes I'll eventually forgive him for.

But he doesn't tell me that.

He kisses my head and murmurs, "Good girl."

And then, all his warmth disappears as he leaves the room and walks out of my life as quickly as he came.

I sink to my knees.

The room closes around me, and my vision blurs as I crawl to my bed and search for my phone. Thomas answers on the first ring. "For the hundredth time, Fallon, we'll be fine while you're gone. Ansel requested the extra days off—"

I don't let him finish.

I just start weeping.

"I'm on my way. Don't hang up."

The following days pass by in a blur.

I exist on autopilot. Thomas drives me to work each morning and home every night. He walks me upstairs, cooks dinner for me or has it delivered, and sits with me while I stare at my food. He's patient while I check my phone every few minutes, sits quietly while I reiterate how I don't understand what happened, and listens to me cry.

"You did nothing wrong," he reminds me for the dozenth time when I break down all over again.

I blame myself constantly, wondering if I pushed Fitz too hard to open up and tell me things. I reflect on every conversation we had, bewildered by the misstep somewhere.

I'm left without closure. I'm stuck in an endless cycle of wondering where everything went wrong.

"Silence is the only answer you need," Thomas says, forcing a spoonful of soup into my mouth. "If he wanted to talk to you, he would. If he wanted to explain to you why he chose to end this, he would. He doesn't want to."

"*He* pursued *me*," I remind him. "He showed up to dinner with Ryan, he invited himself to California, he—"

"I *know*," Thomas interrupts quietly. "I know."

I cover myself with another blanket. No matter how often I turn the fireplace on or how many layers of clothing I wear, I can't warm up. When Fitz left, he took all the heat with him.

"Why does it feel like I keep taking two steps back? I barely knew him." I ask, clutching the blanket. It's as if I'm physically trying to keep pieces of my heart from seeping out and soaking through the delicate fabric.

"Because healing isn't linear," Thomas responds softly, gentle in his tone. "One day, you'll breathe easier. Then, it'll hit you all over again. The memories, the texts, the possibilities." His gaze dips to the floor with a deep sigh as if recalling his heartbreaks. "It doesn't ever fully go away, but it does... lessen."

I whisper weakly, "the pain?"

Thomas slightly shakes his head. "The disappointment of what could've been. You fell for the potential, Mads."

A fresh set of tears fall down my cheeks. Thomas is right. Fitz might've avoided every deep conversation I tried to have with him, but we had such potential. I was slowly breaking down his walls, and maybe that's why he pushed me away. Or perhaps I'm making excuses for him because the truth would simply hurt too much.

At the end of the each day, I am the one sitting on the couch, crying over him, and he isn't speaking to me. He's making a conscious choice to not be in my life.

But the realization doesn't ease the pain.

I rest my chin on my knees. "What do I do now?"

Thomas places the bowl of soup on the coffee table and crawls over to me, pulling me into his arms and kissing the top of my head. "You go to California, Fallon. And you slowly try to move on." He wipes the tear falling from my eye. "It's going to hurt like a motherfucker, Mads, but what do I always say?"

I sniffle and rest my head against his chest. "Fallon can do hard things." Referring to myself in the third person is bizarre, but saying his affirmation aloud oddly helps.

"And I'll be here when you inevitably forget that," he promises. "Remember who you are, Fallon."

I try to remember who I was *before* Fitz walked into my store that day. I faced each day with excitement and a gigantic dash of anxiety, but I knew who I was. I didn't waste time on a man. I didn't romanticize a text. My life before him was simple. It might've been a little dull, but it was something I could rely on. I need to be that version of myself again. I need to harden my heart and strengthen my boundaries.

And never let Fitz in again.

*fallon*

T he ridiculously long flight from New Hampshire to California allowed me time to think and process. Since this trip is work-related, it will give me enough of a distraction not to completely break down. It will require me to focus and be my usual, bubbly self.

Weeks ago, I agreed to be a moderator on a panel at the book convention. The topic discusses where authors draw inspiration from when writing their books. I came up with fifteen questions to ask, which should cover the entirety of the panel. I have various sponsor events to attend, including a luncheon with agents and publishers—a perk Ryan secured for me.

Every minute of my time at the book convention will be accounted for. I arranged for some after-convention dinners with people I've become friends with over the last year. I've tried to fill my schedule with little to no free time. I've always been a pro at boxing my feelings and keeping them locked away until I'm ready to face them. And that's how I need to approach this sudden change in my life. But the truth is, I'm struggling to keep it together. The pain of

Fitz's absence is a constant weight on my chest, making it hard to breathe at times.

If I allowed myself to feel it, I would recognize that Fitz had become part of my daily routine over the last two weeks. I looked forward to his texts. I enjoyed seeing him at the store, laughing with Thomas. I was falling for him. I trusted every word he said. I believed we'd fallen into a good rhythm with each other. He was slowly thawing.

But it was all an illusion.

And that's the thought I can't bear to confront.

I've always prided myself on my ability to see through exteriors and actually see the person behind the mask. As puzzling and aloof as Fitz was, I was drawn to the parts of himself he allowed me to see. Every moment spent with him resembled assembling a puzzle; he kept handing me pieces. I didn't realize until he ended things between us that the pieces just weren't fitting. I was forcing corners.

I keep trying to convince myself to despise him. I'm failing miserably at this self-imposed task.

I've tried watching the encouraging videos on TikTok. I nod along when the beautiful, strong women on the other side tell me to move on. I listen to every word they say, including the podcasts they recommend on how to move forward. But how can I do that when each thought is of him?

I believe I'm one breakdown away from the tarot card readers popping up on my feed, promising he'll return.

Throwing myself into work is the only solution, so I find myself standing outside a small café, waiting for a familiar face to join me for a drink before we share an Uber to the hotel where the convention is being held.

An involuntary squirm from the unexpected hand on the small of my back tightens every muscle in my neck. Being touched right now by anyone other than Thomas is akin to being held down and forced to live a nightmare. Physical touch has always been one of my top love languages, but it's something Fitz ruined for me, at least temporarily. I learned to chase the addiction of the feeling his touch brought me.

"Did I scare you?" Ryan asks with his brow furrowed.

I give him my most convincing smile, though even I know it must look fake. "Just tired, I guess. Long trip."

He doesn't buy my excuse, as evidenced by his concerned nod. "Let's get you caffeinated."

The café is quiet, the kind of place where the clink of a spoon against a mug feels like a personal conversation. We stand at the counter, silently reading the menu boards on the wall. I see the words, but I can't focus on them. Instead of ordering a specialty drink, I settle for a plain black coffee.

"So, where are you staying while you're in town?" Ryan asks. "It's in West Hollywood, right?"

I force another smile, finding a place to sit after ordering to stall before answering. "Yes. A boutique hotel. It's... intimate. Very small. Only three floors."

Fitz suggested it, of course. He mentioned the place during one of our conversations, and even though I barely knew him, I respected his taste. He told me it was perfect for someone like me—a quiet, intimate spot to unwind after a long day, with a rooftop bar and pool offering a stunning view of the city. It's tucked away from the city's bustling crowds, much like I'm trying to be in my own life.

My heart tightens, a confusing mix of appreciation and longing stirring inside me. He hadn't just suggested a place to stay. He shared a piece of himself with me, which I didn't think he often did. But why? Why would he do that if he was just passing through my life?

"Intimate," I echo, my voice quieter now. I hate how

much the word feels loaded in my chest. "Fitz suggested it."

Ryan's smile falters just for a moment before he leans in, clearly sensing the shift in my mood. "What's going on?"

The barista brings our drinks to the table and takes the numbered stand, departing once she ensures we need nothing else. I wrap my hands around the warm cup, breathing in the smell of the dark-roasted brew. "We, um…" I trail off, unsure how to explain the last two weeks to Ryan. "I don't know." I huff a dry laugh, unable to stop the water welling in my eyes.

Every interaction with Ryan has always been surface-level. I kept it that way on purpose. Something I'm learning about myself since Fitz walked out of my life is how few people I've allowed in my life since leaving Missouri. I have superficial relationships and keep everyone at a distance as a safeguard. It hasn't made it easy to open up to anyone, but I find myself longing for voices aside from the ones in my head.

Ryan scoots his chair closer to mine. He doesn't touch me this time. I suppose he picked up on my previous reaction. "You can talk to me," he offers softly.

I lick my lips, still tasting the salt from the last time I shed tears over this man. "He's… gone." My voice is raw from how often I've repeated those words. "He blew through my life like a tornado, leaving nothing but destruction behind." I think of his final words to me—how easy I was to destroy. "And it's weird, right? How broken I feel over him?"

He places his arm on the back of my chair, facing me fully. "No, Fallon. It's not weird. He was… intense. I only met him once, but I could tell how enraptured you were with the other. The chemistry was very obvious." He laughs then, slightly shaking his head. "If there's anything

I've learned from working with authors as long as I have and reading their manuscripts, it's how rare a connection with someone is."

I close my eyes to prevent tears from escaping.

"People who don't read say how often books dramatize relationships. They claim no one can exist as fictional characters do. It's bullshit." I hear him take a sip of his drink. "Authors bare their souls on pages to put into words how humans function and exist. Just because you're experiencing something that seems disorienting and foreign doesn't make it any less real. You should know as well as anyone how well fiction mirrors real life. Don't invalidate how you feel just because of the notion that you shouldn't feel the way you do after a short time."

This is the most eloquent I've ever heard Ryan speak. He's put aside the persona he's built to actually empathize with what I'm feeling. It's given me a refreshing outlook on him. And what he's saying to me is making me feel like I'm not crazy. My experience with Fitz and the short time we lived as two souls attempting to merge into one was real.

Those events *did* happen.

I did imagine what it'd be like to have Fitz in my life permanently because he allowed me to do so. He gave me a false sense of security. It's normal for me to be reeling from the loss. More than that, *it's okay.* His time with me might not matter to him, but our time together mattered to *me.*

I shouldn't discount how I feel to compensate for how he might *not* feel. He no longer deserves that much power and control over my emotions.

"Thank you," I whisper, gifting Ryan with an actual, albeit small, smile. "Thank you for listening to me."

He holds his cup up, waiting for me to grab mine and mirror him. "To brighter days," he says, knocking his cup against mine. "We are in California, after all."

"To brighter days," I repeat.

On my last day in California, I make it to the beach. I've dreaded it since Fitz planned for us to visit as many beaches as possible during our trip, but I decided that missing out on something I looked forward to would've been unfair. I planned to go to a beach prior to meeting him. There isn't any reason I shouldn't honor what I longed for.

Ryan stayed by my side for the entire convention. He kept my mind busy and never allowed me to settle. Before this trip, I never looked forward to his visits to Sanderling. Now, I can truly say that I'll enjoy catching up with him. I'll never feel for him what he might wish I did, but I'll never be able to repay him for keeping me afloat when I wanted to sink. He offered to come with me to the beach, but I needed to be alone.

I love being out on the water. During the summer in Sanderling, Thomas rents jet skis for us. Ansel is a boat club member, so he can rent sailboats to take us out. Nearly every evening, when it's warm, and the sunshine glistens on the water, we're out there. Thomas burns easily. I always have to bring two bottles of sunscreen with me, blaming his Irish roots for being so delectable to the sun. Before summer ended, he ordered matching Friends-esque shirts for us. Each shirt has a picture of two lobsters holding claws with the text, 'You're my lobster' printed underneath.

It's the shirt I'm wearing to the beach in Santa Monica when I decide to let Fitz go. I stand along the jagged short, allowing the cold water to brush my toes, and welcome it. I want any feeling aside from the constant fear of never breathing deeply again—the swelling in my chest for every thought of him that crosses my mind.

And as I stare across the open water, still desolate from the departing winter, tears spring to my eyes at the realization of one simple concept. As much as I love the water, as often as I've dreamed of living near it, if there was a sudden lack of it, it would never be worth drowning to prevent its goodbye. And that same theory needed to apply to losing him.

Everything I feel for him is vast and alive, but our wreckage needs to wash away in the waves.

Forever missing.

But never forgotten.

And now, I'm home. Well, at the store. Thomas is closing the registers, Ansel is asking for every detail of my time in California, and none of us thought to lock the door to prevent anyone else from coming in. Not that a lock could even stop someone like the man who breezes through the front like *he's* the one who owns the place.

"What the fuck are you doing here?" Thomas asks.

I squeeze his arm. "It's okay, Thomas." I meet Jace halfway, blocking him from going any further. "We're closed."

Jace sits on the edge of a table, the books sliding a few inches to make room for him. I exercise *extreme* patience while outright glaring at him. "I want to take you to dinner," Jace says, extending his legs and crossing one ankle over the other.

"Um... no?" I'm dumbfounded by the demand.

He picks up one of the books from the table and pretends to flip through it. "Come on, Fallon. It's over between you and Fitz. He won't care if you come to dinner with me."

I resist the urge to snatch the book from his hands and yell for Ansel to escort this cockroach from my store. "I declined once already, Jace. Do I need to repeat myself?"

The corner of his mouth lifts in a smirk. "Ah. You think that a second chance with Fitz won't ever be possible if you come to dinner with me." He drops the book back to its stack. "Here's the beauty of it, Fallon. Fitz knows."

Nausea settles in my stomach. "Excuse me?"

With a nonchalant shrug, Jace stands. "Yeah. I asked him if I could ask you out if things between you didn't work out. He didn't give a fuck." He pulls his phone from his pocket. "I can call him to double-check if you'd like."

My ears start ringing. I truly meant so little to him that he'd willingly let his best friend ask me out? "My answer still stands, Jace. I have no interest in going to dinner with you."

Bravely, since I feel Thomas creeping up behind me, Jace takes my chin between his fingers. "Come on, Fallon. I know you find me attractive. One dinner won't kill you."

I jerk my chin away as Thomas moves between us, shoving Jace back a step and nearly causing him to trip over the table. "No, but I might kill you. Get the fuck out of here."

Jace recovers smoothly, his cocky grin returning as if nothing happened at all. "Text Fitz for my number if you change your mind." He lazily salutes us before exiting.

Thomas follows him to the front door while Ansel appears beside me, gently touching my arm. "Are you okay?"

"No," I breathe. "I'm not. I can't believe how he little he cared about me when I cared so much. I was wrong about everything."

I doubt I will ever be okay again.

"It's strange," I whisper, mindlessly rearranging the table Jace made a mess of. "Fitz was once such a tangible presence in my life to nothing more than a collection of moments." I drag my fingers across the textured front cover and trace the title. "Memories can linger forever in your mind. A particular person can be a phantom for as long as you let them. Do you know how much power that bestows them?"

Thomas reappears beside me, palming the small of my back. "Infinite," he murmurs.

*hayes*

I lean against a wall in my fitted suit, not caring if crossing my arms over my chest will wrinkle the jacket. I was coerced into an engagement photoshoot with Raquel, yet she's somehow been the only one photographed thus far. She hired a makeup artist and had a dress designed for the occasion, going overboard in the extravagant gold sequin dress. She's naturally brunette but has dyed her hair platinum blonde since high school, and it's falling down her back in waves. But the ring signifies the weight of this lie.

My father told her to choose any ring she wanted, and she did. She went to Harry Winston and had one sized immediately, demanding it be ready for this photoshoot. I didn't care to ask how many carats. My only assignment was to show up for the picture and smile, and then I'd be free until the rehearsal dinner, which is coming up too soon for my liking.

None of this is to my liking.

I can't stop thinking about Fallon. She's in my dreams. She lingers in every inhale. It's like the thought of her gives my lungs the strength to function. I was cruel to her on purpose, but the look of betrayal on her face when I left will live with me forever. And no matter how often I try convincing myself that I'm doing all this for her, it's never enough. I could've fought harder. I could've thrown aside my father's empire and risked it all, but that would have left her vulnerable and exposed to my father's vengeance, which he has never been short on. No, this was the quickest solution. With any luck, we can get the marriage annulled once Raquel has the baby. We'll cite irreconcilable differences as the reason.

The sound of camera shutters fills the air as I adjust my shirt collar, frowning when the photographer beckons me forward. The photographer's commands float over me—turn this way, hold her hand like you mean it, look at her like you care—and I do my best to comply. But none of it is real. Not the smile on my face. Not the touch of her hand in mine. It's all part of the performance.

The weight in my chest grows heavier with every minute I spend in front of the camera, and I hate it. I hate being here, dressed in a suit for another woman, acting like I'm a man who has his life together. The truth is, my heart isn't in this. It isn't in any of it. And as much as I try to bury the feelings, the thought of Fallon lingers like an ache I can't shake.

"Come on, Hayes, a little more enthusiasm," the photographer calls, snapping another picture as I stand stiffly, the fake smile frozen on my face. "Show me the love."

"Fitz," Raquel grits through clenched teeth.

I catch my reflection in the mirror behind the photographer, my eyes hollow, my jaw clenched.

What the hell am I doing?

The photographer notices the shift in my energy and steps back, his frown deepening. "Alright, take five," he says, raising his hands in surrender. "I think we're losing the magic."

I walk off to the side, trying to collect my thoughts. Every step feels like I'm sinking deeper into the mire of my own confusion. I didn't expect this to bother me as badly as it is.

I take my phone out of my pocket. The screen lights up with a text from Andrew. He already knows everything.

> How's it going? You know how Frank feels about these shoots—make sure you're making the right impression.

I run my hand over my face, feeling the exhaustion creeping in. How can I make the right impression when all I want to do is throw it all away and focus on something real? Something like Fallon.

But I must go through with it. My father's expectations hang over me like a dark cloud. My obligations are clear.

> I'll need a drink after this.

> Where's Jace? He isn't responding.

> I'll check his location.

I didn't want to share my location with Jace and Andrew, but Jace stole our phones one night and added us to an app that shows where we are on a map and when our phones need to charge. It's juvenile but has worked out when Jace gets too drunk at a bar and requires us to pick him up, which is often.

> Well. You won't like this.

> Fuck. Where is he?

> He's in Sanderling.

At Fallon's store.

I freeze, my breath catching in my throat. The words are like a punch to the gut. The rest of the world seems to blur around me as I reread it, the message sinking deeper.

I've always known Jace has no boundaries, but this... This is something else entirely. He's going to Sanderling to *pursue* Fallon? After everything? He knows what I had put on the line. Yet, he's going to try to steal her away, make a mockery of everything we had—or maybe it's just a game to him.

I didn't believe he'd actually follow through on our deal.

My heart pounds in my ears. No. Not like this. Not now. Fallon can't find out like this.

I don't even think twice. I turn, ignoring the photographer and Raquel, and grab my jacket, storming out of the shoot. The cold air slaps me in the face as I walk quickly to my motorcycle. The idea of Jace and Fallon together ignites something in me. I am going to stop this. I don't need to think about it. I don't need permission. I just need to get to her.

I skid to a stop in the parking lot of Shoreline Scribes, the engine of my motorcycle roaring as I slam it into park. My chest is tight with anger and something darker, a raw ache I can't ignore anymore.

Jace's silver car is parked just a few spaces away, and there he is—leaning against it like he owns the place, a cocky grin on his face as he looks at the storefront.

He sees me before I can get a word out. His grin only widens, his eyes full of amusement. "Well, if it isn't the prodigal son himself."

Without thinking, I march toward him and punch him square in the jaw. The satisfying crack of contact rings in my ears as he staggers back, holding his face but still smirking.

"Stay the hell away from Fallon," I spit, my voice low, dripping with venom.

Jace wipes his lip, tasting the blood from the corner of his mouth. His smirk falters just for a moment before it returns with renewed mischief. "I don't want her, Fitz. Not in the way you think."

I blink, confused. "What the hell are you talking about?"

He leans back, folding his arms, his expression turning serious for once. "I was testing her to see if she'd be loyal to you--if she's as into you as you think she is."

My throat tightens, and I fight to keep my composure. "Testing her?" I growl, taking a step forward, the distance between us narrowing. "You went to her, put her through some game to see if she'd fall for it?"

"I wasn't trying to screw with her," Jace says, his voice more level now, almost calculating. "I wanted to see if she'd turn me down. And she did, Fitz. She turned me down flat. Not even a second thought."

A surge of relief floods through me before it's quickly replaced by something else—something deeper. The tension leaves my body, but I feel it again, stronger than ever.

"And now I see it," Jace continues, his eyes searching mine with a strange intensity. "You *are* in love with her, aren't you?"

I stagger back, blinking rapidly, trying to process what he said. "What? No."

Jace laughs bitterly. "You're willing to risk your father's wrath to leave an engagement shoot for a woman you barely know? *That* is what love looks like, Fitz. It's not the bullshit with the girl your father chose for you. It's the one you'll drop everything for. The one you can't stand to see with someone else, even your best friend. You have never reacted this way with anyone else. You're in love with her."

I stand there, frozen, as his words sink deeper than I ever expected. The truth is staring me in the face, and I can't deny it anymore. I *am* in love with Fallon. And I've risked everything I'd built up with my family and my obligations to ensure her dreams don't slip through her fingers.

The weight of everything comes crashing down on me. I don't feel in control for the first time in a long while. It's been Fallon in control this entire time. Fallon is the one who has me in the palm of her hand.

The first time I've been in love with someone, and we can't even be together. I realized it too late. I made a deal with the devil for her.

"Is she…" Trailing off, I turn from Jace to look at the front door of Shoreline Scribes. Even if she is still inside, it doesn't matter. There's nothing I could say right now to fix this. "What did you say to her, Jace?"

Jace opens his car door. "I told her you wouldn't care if I asked her out. Even then, she still showed no interest."

"You fucking prick," I mutter, shoving a hand through my hair. "This was a fucked up way to go about testing her loyalty or whatever you claim it was for. I didn't need confirmation, Jace. She's already told me I'm all she wants."

"That wasn't why I did it, Fitz." He waits for me to face him again before he continues. "You walk through life pretending you don't give a shit about anyone. Even us. And I know why that is. Believe me, if anyone understands, it's me. But it's all bullshit."

I head toward my bike. "I don't need to fucking hear this from you, Jace."

"Yeah, walk away, Fitz. But you can't keep avoiding

every feeling you have forever, man." Jace slides into the driver seat of his car. "Eventually, it's going to catch up with you because you're not your father."

I pause, then turn slowly.

Jace is leaning back in his seat, one leg inside the car and the other casually stretched out. "Ah, that caught your attention, didn't it?" He pulls a lighter from his jacket pocket and lights a joint. He keeps a stash in his middle console. "You tried for years to convince yourself you can be the next Frank Fitzgerald. You want to be callous. You want to disregard anyone who might care about you."

I hate to admit I'm listening to him.

He spins the joint between his fingers. "You're your mother, Fitz. You run instead of facing the feelings you *do* have. And if you keep that up, you'll be running forever, just like her."

I clench my fists, perturbed by how casually he's goading me. "I'm not either of my parents."

Jace inserts himself fully into his car, the joint dangling from the corner of his mouth. "No?" He starts the car, then leaves me with one final demand before closing the door. "Prove it."

*hayes*

The hum of conversation fills the banquet hall, each step I take feels heavier than the last. The golden lights cast a warm glow on the tables and the guests, all with their bright smiles and polished exteriors. But they are not the reason I'm here. After ending things with Fallon, I wasn't planning to come. I know she doesn't want to see me, but I don't care.

The weight of my emotions is suffocating because one thing is undeniably clear: I am in love with her.

I want another chance to see her, even if I can't be with her. I want to make sure she's okay. I want to see that fire in her eyes again, the strength she carries with her, the way she makes everything feel real. I've come a long way from the person I used to be, and it's all because of her. And as I scan the room, I find her.

She's standing across the hall, bathed in the soft light, a vision in an emerald green dress that seems to shimmer every time she moves. Made of only silk, it exposes her delicate shoulders and collarbone, which no longer show the bruising of my teeth. Because of the plunging neckline, the slightest glimpse of her soft breasts is revealed on either side. And the slit in her skirt, *my god,* displays the inner part of her left thigh, drawing my gaze higher until her skin disappears behind the fabric, leaving me yearning for just another inch.

Her long raven hair is curled, leaving her profile framed in an exquisite composite of confidence and ease, and for a moment, I can't breathe. She's stunning. No, more than stunning—she's everything I've been trying to fight my entire life.

I hold my breath and silence the noise of bystanders chatting to focus solely on her. The heat of my gaze could warm cities, perhaps even set her aflame from where she stands on the opposite side of the banquet hall.

It is certainly enough to draw her attention.

Her green eyes glow like sapphires in the twinkling lights, holding me in place and clutching my heart until I'm positive I've stopped breathing.

Fallon.

I want to walk over to her. I need to talk to her. To apologize for everything, to explain the mess I had made of things. But before I can move, I feel a presence beside me.

Raquel.

My father insisted I bring her. It was the only way to ensure I would be the one to present the grant tonight.

She loops her arm through mine, pulling me back to reality. "Hayes," she says, her smile dripping with sweetness that doesn't reach her eyes. "You can't avoid me all night."

I ignore her, remaining fixated on Fallon, who has since turned away from me after noticing Raquel on my arm.

Some part of me hoped that Raquel didn't actually go to my father—that she wouldn't be okay trapping me into a marriage I want no part of. But similarly to me, Raquel would rather not face her father's wrath. It's archaic to think about. She's terrified to tell her father she's pregnant because of what his reaction might be. For that, I do empathize with her. But I disagree that I should bear responsibility.

I attempt to pry my arm away from Raquel's death grip. Raised in the same world as me, Raquel is all about appearances. I imagine she's murdering me internally for not keeping up our charade well enough in public, especially since most people here know who I am. Fallon hasn't realized it yet because she hasn't been involved in the business world long enough to know her enemies.

I'm frantic for her.

Even with Raquel still stuck to me like glue, I cross the banquet hall, nodding to Thomas when he sees me approach. He nudges Fallon and whispers something to her, taking her hand before she spins around to face me.

I look at no one but her.

There's so much I need to say to her.

"Fallon," I say, her name like sweet nectar on my lips. "You look beautiful tonight." I might be drooling. "Radiant."

"Fitz," she mirrors. I see no hatred in how she looks at me. Even if she did despise me, nothing would've stopped me from coming tonight. "Thank you."

Thomas doesn't let me off as easily. "What the fuck are you even doing here? Do you own a small business?"

Raquel laughs. I'd forgotten she's here. "How do you not know who he is? This is Hayes Fitzgerald."

Ansel balks. "Okay, and?"

"That isn't the last name you wrote down on your paperwork," Thomas says, folding his arms over his chest. "Who the fuck are you?"

Fallon raises an unimpressed eyebrow, which causes me to grin. And to my surprise, I don't care that Raquel is about to give away my identity. It no longer matters. I secured Fallon's future for her. That is all that's important.

I want to kiss her. I need to see if she tastes the same. I'm not holding back at the blatant way I'm admiring everything she is from head to toe and back again. But she doesn't squirm under my gaze. Even after I was a bastard to her, she still doesn't lack confidence in who she is around me.

Raquel releases my arm and turns, searching the room. When she spots FFJ's banner displayed on stage, she points to it and looks over her shoulder at Thomas. "His dad owns half of FFJ Holdings. Hayes will be the CEO someday."

Fallon's eyes dart from the sign back to me, her lips parting as surprise melts into an otherwise disinterested expression. And I can see the wheels in her mind turning as she connects the dots—my condo in Sanderling, why I never asked for a paycheck, how I could afford such a luxurious lifestyle.

"That's the business you told me about?" she asks quietly.

Solemnly, I nod.

Raquel spins on her heel to face us again fully, but when she places her hand on her stomach, Fallon's gaze lowers. And then, she pales as she blurts out, "You're pregnant."

Fuck. Fuck, fuck.

Fallon tried to warn me about this once—her ability to tell when a woman is pregnant. I didn't consider this when I made the impromptu decision to still attend the banquet.

Raquel's hand flies up to cover her mouth as her other grips my arm. "Oh, am I already showing? It's so early! The doctor said I wouldn't be able to tell for weeks." Raquel looks at me, laughing as she adds, "Hopefully we'll be married before there's a bump."

"Married," Fallon rasps, backing away a step, her gaze immediately snagging on Raquel's left hand. Her eyes no longer shine from the light but from tears. "Of course. Excuse me, I need to go to the restroom."

I approach Fallon to explain that the child Raquel is carrying isn't mine, that I don't want to marry her, that I have no feelings toward Raquel at all, but Thomas steps between us. "I think you've done enough," he says, his voice laced with warning.

"Thomas," I plead. "I can explain—"

From the speaker, the event organizer instructs everyone to take their seats for the program to begin. I look around the hall for Fallon, but she was quick to disappear. I'll present the check quickly and insist she speak to me afterward.

I take my place at the podium, trying to ignore the buzz of discomfort in my chest. It doesn't help that the weight of Fallon's absence in the audience presses down on me harder than anything else in the room.

I clear my throat. "Good evening, everyone," I begin, my voice steady but distant. "My name is Hayes Fitzgerald, and I'm the son of Frank Fitzgerald, CEO of FFJ Holdings. Tonight, we are honored to be one of the sponsors of this event, supporting the wonderful businesses that make Sanderling such a special place."

I scan the crowd for a glimpse of Fallon. It isn't hard to miss her, but she isn't here. She isn't anywhere. I can't find her in the sea of faces.

The room quiets, and I force myself to continue. "This year, we're proud to present the small business grant to a local favorite: Shoreline Scribes."

There's applause, but it feels distant—like I'm not even part of the moment. I look down at the stage and continue, "Fallon Madison, the owner of Shoreline Scribes, couldn't be with us tonight, but we are thrilled to support her incredible work. She has built something truly special here, and this grant will help her continue that vision as she expands into the heart of the city."

I pause, waiting for the applause to subside, my heart pounding as I search the room one last time. Fallon isn't here. And I can't help but wonder if she's gone for good.

Thomas stands from his chair and steps forward, but I shake my head. "Since Fallon isn't here to accept," I say quickly, "I'll be hand-delivering the check to Shoreline Scribes personally. I want to make sure Fallon gets it directly from me."

Thomas shoots me a look of irritation, maybe even confusion, but he doesn't argue. He can't, really. Not here in front of hundreds of people. I see the frustration in his eyes as he turns to walk away, but I don't care. I'm not letting Fallon slip away this time. Not without a fight.

***

The sun is barely peeking over the horizon as I arrive at Shoreline Scribes the next morning, the store's quaint, familiar façade standing in stark contrast to the turmoil inside me. I can't wait any longer to see Fallon. After everything at the banquet, I can't stand the thought of leaving things unresolved.

She wasn't home last night when I tried to stop by. She wasn't at the studio. And I never found out where Thomas lives, so I couldn't check there.

I park my motorcycle outside, the engine's hum barely registering as I remove my helmet and walk toward the door. The weight of the check in my jacket pocket feels like lead, but it isn't just about the money. I have to explain. I have to make things right.

I push open the door, the familiar bell chiming as I enter the store. The smell of coffee and books greets me—

so *her*—but the place is empty. Only the soft shuffle of papers behind the counter breaks the silence. I look around for Fallon, but she isn't here.

Instead, Thomas is at the counter, organizing a stack of books, his brow furrowed in concentration. When he sees me, his gaze hardens, but he doesn't say anything. He knows exactly why I'm here.

"Where is she?" I ask, my voice tight with both frustration and urgency. "I need to see her."

Thomas doesn't immediately respond. He takes his time, placing the papers down with a deliberate slowness that only increases my impatience.

"She's not here," Thomas says finally, his voice flat. "She left after the banquet. She's fine."

I feel a rush of relief and confusion. "Where did she go?" I press, stepping closer, the words tumbling out before I can stop them. "I need to talk to her. I need to explain about Raquel, about everything."

Thomas gives me a cold look, his arms crossing over his chest. "You're really going to tell her now? After all this time?"

My throat tightens, the weight of the situation pressing in on me. "Thomas, please, just tell me where she is. I need to clear things up. I need her to know that Raquel's baby isn't mine. I wasn't with anyone else when I was with Fallon."

I can see the muscle in Thomas's jaw tighten. He stares at me momentarily, sizing me up, before shaking his head. "I'm not the one who needs to hear that," he says, his voice quiet but firm. "She deserves to hear it from you, Fitz. But I don't think you'll get that chance if you don't know where she's gone."

I step back, suddenly unsure of everything. "What do you mean? Where did she go?"

Thomas hesitates for a moment before answering, his voice barely audible. "She went home. To Missouri."

I freeze. "Home?" I repeat, my voice cracking. Her home is here. Her home is near me. "You mean... her hometown? But why? Is she visiting her parents?"

Thomas doesn't look at me as he says, "Her parents died over a year ago, Fitz."

The world seems to stop. My heart stutters in my chest, and for a moment, I can't breathe. I try to process what he just said, but the words don't make sense. Her parents... died.

She always talked about them like they were alive. All the stories she told me didn't imply they had died. But the darkness she always carried with her was because of this.

The room tilts around me, the weight of it all crashing down. I knew Fallon had some kind of pain buried deep inside, but I never knew it was like this. And now, here I am—too late to be there for her and offer my support when she needs it most.

I swallow hard, trying to find my voice again. "I didn't know. I didn't know about her parents."

Thomas's gaze softens, but he still doesn't offer any sympathy. "She doesn't talk about it much. She never has. But this is why she's been avoiding you, Fitz. She's been dealing with her grief, and then you come into the picture... You have no idea how much you've shaken her up."

I can feel my chest tightening again, and my thoughts are a chaotic mess. *I didn't know.* I didn't know about her parents, her grief, the weight she had been carrying all this time. All I've been concerned about is my own mess and lies.

"Is she going to stay there for a while?" I ask, already knowing the answer but desperate to hear it. "Maybe take some time away from everything?"

Thomas looks at me, his eyes cold. "She's gone to her parents' graves for the first time since their funerals. She's been burying her grief and unable to face it. I don't think she'll be coming back any time soon."

I inhale deeply to try and slow my heart rate, my mind reeling. She's gone. She left, not just from the banquet, but from Sanderling. From me. And now, I have to deal with the consequences.

I turn toward the door, every part of me aching to follow her, to ensure she doesn't shut me out completely. But I stop before I can take another step.

"Thomas," I say, my voice softer now. "I need to see her. Please. Tell me where she is. I need to apologize. I need to make things right."

The hardness in expression dissolves. "It's not that simple, Fitz. You've got a lot to fix. And I'm not sure you're ready for what that will take."

I don't answer him. I don't know what to say. All I can think about is Fallon and how I've failed her—hurt her when she's already been through so much.

"Thomas, I'm in love with her." I say the words aloud for the first time, knowing, without a doubt, just how true they are. "Please help me fix this. Tell me where she is."

Thomas doesn't say anything for a full minute. I understand what I'm asking from him. I don't deserve his trust anymore, but he must sense my desperation because he finally says, "I'll text you the address of where she's staying."

I book the next flight out.

*fallon*

The wind howls through the cemetery, a mournful whisper that carries the scent of damp earth and cold steel. I stand in front of their graves, my parents' names etched in simple, cold stone—like something you might see on a monument to a stranger.

But they weren't strangers. They were my parents. And standing here, staring at their names carved into the earth, I feel the hollow ache of their absence, a raw wound that has never quite healed.

It's been just over a year since I buried them. A year since I last saw their faces, heard their voices, felt their warmth. It doesn't feel like enough time has passed. I still expect to see my mom's soft, reassuring smile when I enter a room. I still find myself wishing I could ask my dad for advice, for reassurance. Every day feels like I'm walking through life without a map or direction, and I hate it.

I hate the emptiness in my chest. I hate how the grief has become a constant companion, lingering in the corners of my mind, wrapping itself around me like a cloak I can't escape.

There were times, right after it happened, when I

didn't even know how to breathe. I was suffocating in the thick fog of my own guilt, my own self-loathing. I had begged them to pick me up that night, my graduation night, when I should've been celebrating with friends. I'd been drunk. I should've known better. I should've never called them.

But I had. I called them, and they came. They died because of me.

The thought still hits me like a wave crashing against the shore, pulling me under, suffocating me. The guilt is always there, like an anchor at the bottom of my soul, dragging me into the depths.

I blink rapidly, forcing myself to breathe. My chest feels tight like the air in this cemetery is made of lead, pressing down on me. My fingers tremble as I wipe my eyes, hoping the cold wind will dry them faster than my hands can.

It was easy to forget about the pain, to ignore the fact that I couldn't breathe when I was with Fitz. When I was with him, the world felt different. It felt brighter. He had a way of turning my brain off—making me forget everything that hurt. He made me feel alive again like I hadn't felt since that night. He made me forget my parents for a while, forget my grief, forget everything that was suffocating me.

I fell for him so quickly. Too quickly, I realize now. But it wasn't just the way he looked at me. It wasn't just his smile or voice that made my heart race. It was the way he made me feel like I could breathe again. The way he gave me a moment to escape the pain, to escape the guilt that never left.

He became an addiction. A temporary fix to the constant ache inside me. When I was with him, I could forget the sadness. I could forget that I had no idea how to live without my parents. But that was the problem, wasn't it?

I clung to him like a lifeline. I clung to him so tightly because he made me feel something other than the weight of the grief that threatened to swallow me whole. I fell for him too fast, too recklessly, because I was desperate for anything that could make the world stop spinning for just a moment. I jumped into his warmth because it was easier than dealing with the cold inside me.

But it was never going to be enough. I knew that from the start. Fitz wasn't the solution to my pain. He couldn't heal the wound I had carried for so long, no matter how much I wished he could.

I inhale deeply, steadying myself against the gust of wind that sweeps through the cemetery. The grave markers are cold beneath my fingertips, and the earth feels heavy around me as if trying to remind me that my parents are gone. Gone forever. I have to accept that. I have to let go of the guilt and the fear. I have to stop holding on to the past and start figuring out how to live in the present.

But it isn't that simple. Not for me.

I've pushed so many people away and kept them at arm's length because I'm terrified of losing them like I've lost my parents. The thought of getting close to someone, of letting them in, makes my chest tighten with panic. I can't do that again. I can't bear to feel that kind of pain again.

But with Fitz, it felt different. With him, I convinced myself that I could let go of the fear. Perhaps I could let myself fall.

And now, after everything that happened and went wrong, I'm not sure I can handle losing him too.

I'm not sure I can survive that.

But she's pregnant. The woman he was with at the banquet, that beautiful woman, is carrying his child. Since meeting her, I've imagined a hundred different scenarios, but each ends similarly.

Fitz is gone, too. Some part of me still hoped he'd come back—that he'd run into the store with apologies and explanations. But not even a text came through to warn me that there was someone else—that I might someday meet her and learn of their child.

And now, I need to let him go, too.

Maybe we'll meet again someday, five years from now, when our lives are put together.

I'll tell him how desperately in love with him I was. Baring my soul to him still wouldn't be enough to convey how each breath I took was achingly, soul-crushingly tied to his. How I noticed our steps were always in-sync.

How I would've willingly gone to my grave trying to break down his walls. I would've crawled there myself, nails dugs into the dirt, knees bruised and scraped if it meant he realized how miserable I was without him.

Like he took a piece of me that he never returned. It'll live within him forever. Blood gushing, unstitched.

I'll tell him. Even if we only cross paths for a moment. If it's the last tick of a watch, only seconds with him, I promise he'll know how dearly I needed him.

Even if the world is crumbling around us, he'll know.

I look down at the graves again, the words on the stones blurring as the tears threaten to spill over once more. It was easier to be angry at myself than to accept the truth—that they were gone and nothing could bring them back. Not Fitz. Not anyone.

The wind picks up again, and I turn my face into it, letting the cold sting my skin. I need to clear my head, find a way to move on and breathe again.

Just as I'm about to turn and walk away, I freeze. My heart skips a beat. I know this feeling. The one that prickles my skin, the one that makes me feel like I'm not alone anymore.

I turn slowly, and there he is—standing at the edge of

the cemetery, his silhouette outlined against the pale sky. Fitz.

His presence hits me like a shockwave, his eyes locking on mine even from a distance. He stands still, waiting for me to make the first move as if he isn't sure he should approach me.

I don't know what to say. My heart is racing, and my emotions are a chaotic mess of confusion and longing.

I've never wanted to see anyone more than I want to see him now. But I'm not ready to face him. Not yet. Not when everything inside me is so tangled up in him and my fear.

He starts to move toward me, his footsteps slow but purposeful. I feel the ground shift beneath me as he closes the distance, and before I can even catch my breath, he's standing in front of me. He's so close that I can feel his warmth and smell the faint trace of his cologne.

"I didn't know where else to go," he says quietly, his voice rough. "I've been looking for you. I… I had to see you."

I swallow hard, the words sticking in my throat. "Why?" I manage to ask, my voice barely above a whisper.

"Because I couldn't leave things the way they were," he says, his eyes searching mine. "And I… I'd like to know what happened to them. I wish you would've told me, Fallon."

I wipe the tears from my cheeks with the palm of my hand. "Honesty has never been our strong suit, Hayes."

It's the first time I've ever called him that. Hayes Fitzgerald—the son of the billionaire Frank Fitzgerald. I googled them on the flight over. FFJ Holdings has its own stock, for God's sake. That's how large their corporation is. And I was concerned about how much I paid Fitz for moving a few boxes around. "Speaking of, I have so many questions."

"So do I." He gestures behind me at the headstones. "What happened to them, Fallon?"

I shake my head slowly as tears roll down my cheeks. "I can't… I can't tell you. You'll think I'm awful." I inhale a stuttering breath. "They died because of me."

"Fallon," he says gently, but his voice comes out rough like he can't believe the implication. He reaches out, his hand hovering momentarily before placing it on my shoulder. I flinch slightly at the contact, but I don't pull away. "I promise you that's impossible. I'd like your side of the story."

I brace for the inevitable conclusion he'll draw about me, and I let him in on the secret I've carried around silently for far too long.

"I was at a bar with my friends that night—graduation night, you know?" My voice trembles as I speak, my hands wringing before me. "We were celebrating, just drinking and acting like we had the whole world ahead of us. But I drank too much. Way too much."

I swallow hard, closing my eyes for a moment. The memories are still too painful to relive. "I wasn't thinking straight, and I promised my dad I'd always call him if I needed a ride home. So, I did. I called them, and they showed up, laughing like they always did." A faint smile crosses my face, but it quickly falters. "My mom was trying to sing along with me as we drove off, and my dad kept making jokes about how loud I was. It was supposed to be a funny, happy memory, but it isn't anymore."

I pause, staring into the distance, and my shoulders slump. "As we were pulling out of the parking lot, there was this drunk guy—he was leaving at the same time. He got into his truck, but he wasn't paying attention. He hit the gas too hard, and before we even knew what happened, he rammed right into our car." My voice cracks, and I take a shaky breath, my hands clenching into fists as the moment hits me again. "The impact was so much stronger than I ever could have imagined. My parents didn't survive."

My gaze drops to my trembling hands. "I woke up in the hospital hours later, and the doctor told me they were gone. I've never stopped blaming myself, Hayes." My voice is barely a whisper now, the weight of my confession hanging in the air between us. "If I hadn't been so drunk or if I hadn't called them, maybe they'd still be here."

My chest tightens, and I look up at him, my eyes brimming with unshed tears. "It's hard to look at myself and not feel like I'm the reason they died. After that night, I couldn't face what happened, so I left. I cut off all my friends, let a realtor handle selling my childhood home, and never looked back."

When I look at Fitz, I expect to see the same look on his face that everyone gave me after their deaths—pity. But instead, he's looking at me with nothing but understanding. "Fallon… it's not your fault."

I swallow while shaking my head, words unable to form. A sob escapes me, and I wrap my hand around my throat, trying to soothe the burning. It is my fault. It has to be.

"Fallon, listen to me." He steps closer and grips my shoulders tight enough to hold my attention. "What happened to them is horrible. I know it's difficult to understand, but you did not cause that accident. You didn't ask for it to happen."

"It should've been me," I whisper weakly.

"Fuck, Fallon, no." He pulls me into him, his arms enveloping me. "Imagine if they had lost you, Fallon. Imagine the guilt they'd feel for your death. They still would've died that day. They'd be alive, yes, but not living." He presses his lips against my hair. "Don't ever think that again, Fallon."

"You don't think I'm broken?" I ask, my voice small, fearing he will see me differently once the weight of my grief becomes clear.

He pulls away to lift my chin, wiping the tears from my cheeks. "No, Fallon. You're not broken. You're hurting. You've been through hell, and you're still standing. That's not a weakness. That's strength."

"You don't know what it's like," I whisper, my voice filled with vulnerability. "To carry that guilt, to feel like you're responsible for something that should never have happened. The night we went to the jazz lounge was the first time I've touched alcohol since that night. I just… I felt safe with you."

He leans in, his forehead almost touching mine, and for a moment, everything else fades away. It's just the two of us, standing on the edge of something unspoken, something raw.

"I don't know what it's like to lose my parents like you did," he admits softly. "But I know what it's like to carry pain. And I know it's not easy to let it go. But you have to, Fallon. You have to forgive yourself."

I realize, more than ever, how much I needed to hear those words. How much I need to believe them. Fitz is right—this isn't what my parents would want for me. They wouldn't want me carrying the shame for eternity. They were the brightest lights in my life. They worked hard to give me a life they believed I deserved. For them, I need to try to move on. For them, I need to take a step forward instead of constantly looking back and wishing it had been different. But that day… I will forever carry it with me, but it's up to me to decide how much weight it holds.

Fitz brushes his thumb against my cheek. "It's cold," he says, though the chilly temperature in Missouri is nothing compared to what we deal with in New Hampshire. The implication that he's freezing almost makes me laugh.

But I nod, still unsure why he came all this way. I doubt it was for a comforting hug. "If you're hungry, I know a place."

From the inside pocket of his coat, he pulls out a single long stem rose and places it on the stone behind me. The small, intimate gesture brings new tears to my eyes, but he doesn't allow the moment to linger.

Instead, he turns to me, wraps an arm around my shoulders, and leads me away.

*fallon*

The air in the small café is thick with the smell of roasted coffee beans and the soft hum of quiet conversations. The sun has begun to set outside, casting a warm, golden glow through the windows. I sit across from Hayes, my hands trembling and cold, though I try to keep them steady as I cradle my coffee cup, my fingers wrapped around it to steady the storm of emotions brewing inside me.

I want to know how he found me—how he *always* seems to find me. Appearing in places where I am has become a habit of his, and I've become curious just how long he's been following me around.

His presence *here*, though, is surreal. This café is a place where I spent afternoons after school sometimes, laughing with a group of close friends—friends I've since cut off since leaving Missouri. I recognize some faces but no one approaches us. I wouldn't know how to react if they did.

Hayes is quiet, watching me closely, his gaze steady but full of something I can't quite name. I still feel the weight of his words from earlier, his promise that he wants to explain everything. But now, as we sit together, the silence between us is heavy, and I'm unsure how I'm supposed to feel. A part of him is still closed off and hidden from me.

I sip my coffee, and Hayes finally speaks, breaking the stillness. "I know this has been confusing, Fallon," he begins, his voice low, almost apologetic. "Raquel and I… we have a history. We dated once, if that's what to even define it as, but it was never love. It was more of an expectation. An obligation to our families."

"An obligation?" I ask, keeping my voice lowered. "You're telling me you're with her because your family expects it?"

Hayes nods slowly, his eyes briefly darting down to his hands before meeting mine again. "Yeah. Raquel and I were always meant to be a business arrangement. But I never wanted that. I didn't want her. And I sure as hell don't want this marriage." He pauses, his voice heavy with the weight of everything unsaid. "But I have no choice."

I stare at him, unable to process the depth of what he's saying. My heart beats so loudly in my chest that I can barely hear his words. "But why come to me? Why are you telling me all of this now, Hayes?"

He leans back in his chair, his expression pained. "Because I can't keep lying to you, Fallon. Not anymore." He pulls a check from his pocket and slides it across the table. "I didn't persuade any shareholders to vote for you. They were impressed with everything you've done for Sanderling. The community, the store, everything. They saw your vision. You earned that grant."

I don't touch the check. I don't even glance at it. I have no interest in money tainted with secrets from the man I fell in love with.

He meets my gaze, his voice a little softer. "And as for your application for the retail space? My father withdrew FFJ's application. That's why it took so long for yours to be approved. He was the one holding you back. He wanted me to get close to you, to prevent you from expanding. You've rattled him."

My breath catches in my throat as the realization hits me. All this time, I've been fighting so hard for a dream I didn't even know was being sabotaged by the people I thought were helping me. "Why didn't you tell me all of this before?" I ask, my voice shaking with frustration, hurt, and confusion. "Why did you let me think you felt something for me?"

Hayes doesn't answer right away. He looks at me, his gaze searching like he's trying to find the right words. "I wanted to tell you. I've wanted to tell you for so long. But I couldn't, Fallon. I was trapped. My father holds all the cards, and I'm not in a position to make any decisions without his approval. If I don't follow through with this marriage and don't do what he expects, people will be hurt."

His eyes darken with regret. "It's not just about me, Fallon. It's about everyone else who depends on me. I don't have the luxury of making choices that affect just me."

As much as I can empathize with him, I can't help but feel a deep sense of betrayal. All this time, I believed in him. Believed in us. But how could I when his entire life had been dictated by someone else? "And what about us?" I ask, the words slipping out before I can stop them. "What about me, Hayes? What about what we had? Was any of it real?"

His expression softens, and for the first time, I see the vulnerability in his eyes that I haven't noticed before. "It was real, Fallon. Everything between us was real. But I can't ask you to understand what I've been through and still going through. I can't ask you to wait while I'm tied to all this... obligation."

Tears pool in my eyes, but I blink them back, trying to hold myself together. "So, what now? You're just going to walk away and marry her? You're going to go back to your life, and I'm supposed to just accept it?"

He stands suddenly, his chair scraping against the floor. "I wish I could change things. I wish I could fix it all and make it right. But I can't, Fallon. I can't change what I've already done."

He walks toward the door but then pauses to face me one last time. "I'm not asking for you to forgive me. I know I haven't earned that. But I just…" He quiets then, then allows the smallest of grins to lift the corner of his mouth. "I cannot live without my life. I cannot live without my soul."

And then, he's gone, again leaving me to dissect the meaning behind all he said. To give him credit, I believe it's the *most* he's said in all our time together.

"I cannot live without my life," I repeat slowly. Wuthering Heights. He just quoted something Heathcliff said after Catherine's death. It's something he said in grief, unable to cope with the absence of her in his life. He was haunted by the loss of her.

Fuck, that's the most romantic, tragic thing he's ever said to me.

But if that's how he feels about me, if the loss of us, if the loss of *me*, in his life brings him so much pain, there's more to the story than what he's telling me.

Something isn't sitting right. He came all this way, put himself through all of this… to explain, to reveal parts of his life I never knew existed. He's hiding something from me. I know it. And if I'm ever going to understand the whole picture, I need answers. I need to know what's happening behind all the secrecy and obligations. Fitz freed me from my guilt.

It's time to repay the favor.

The plane ride back to New Hampshire was long, but I couldn't stop thinking about everything Hayes had said. It's a tangled web of family, obligation, and sacrifice. But I need to know more. I need to understand why he's willing to destroy everything and why he was willing to let us go.

I find myself walking into the FFJ offices after commandeering Thomas' car for a drive to Boston, looking for anyone who could help me. Hell, I'll seek out Frank Fitzgerald himself if necessary. Thomas wanted to tag along, insisted, really, but I need to learn how to do things on my own. I'll never move on if I don't.

I spot Andrew in the lobby, coming out of the elevator, and my heart skips a beat. I don't waste time walking up to him. "Andrew," I say, my voice tight with determination, "you need to explain to me what's really going on. All of it."

Andrew pauses, his brow furrowing in confusion. "Fallon, what are you doing here?"

"I need the truth," I say, my voice shaking with frustration. "I need you to tell me everything. You *owe* me that."

He looks around as if trying to decide whether to tell me. Finally, sighing, he leads me to a quieter lobby area. "Fitz made a deal with his father, Fallon," he says quietly. "If he marries Raquel, Frank agreed to stop pursuing the location in Sanderling and leave you alone. Raquel's father is the majority owner of FFJ Holdings. Hayes didn't want any part of this, but he's been backed into a corner. He risks losing everything if he doesn't follow through with the marriage."

My chest tightens. "He did this for me?"

Andrew nods. "Exactly. Hayes is stuck, Fallon. He never should have been put in this position. He's been forced into making a decision he didn't want to make. And that's why he hasn't been able to tell you everything."

My knees might give out. Hayes is sacrificing his future

to ensure I have mine. He's willing to live in a forced marriage to allow me my future without his father trying to destroy it. "He loves me," I say aloud as realization dawns on me. His distance and avoidance... it's the recipe for running from anything real.

God, it's like when the boys on the playground torture you because they have a crush on you. Why couldn't he just share this information with me? We could've found a solution instead of him sacrificing his entire future.

"I need to stop this. I need to stop him from making this sacrifice." My fists clench at my sides. "Where is Frank's office?"

Andrew hesitates for a moment before telling me. I won't waste another second. I storm out of the lobby and take the elevator up to the top floor, my heart pounding in my chest as I prepare to confront the man who has forced Hayes into this impossible situation. The only problem is that FFJ's offices are massive and make me feel like I'm in a maze.

I'm about to ask the secretary at the front desk where to locate Frank, but I feel a hand on the small of my back gently guiding me toward a door on the left. Andrew is trailing behind me, but Jace is leading me away.

"He was meeting me for lunch," Andrew informs me. "He saw you get on the elevator and wants to help."

"That doesn't sound like Jace," I mutter.

"I might owe you an apology," Jace says, though his smugness is still very prominent. "To be honest, Fitz has needed someone like you in his life for a long time."

"You do owe me an apology." I give him a small, hesitant smile. I know Fitz left me for reasons bigger than what I can understand right now, but it has shaken how easily I trust people, and Jace hasn't given me many reasons to believe anything he says. But that doesn't mean I need to completely harden my heart against others. "Thank you," I say softly. "I've needed him, too."

Jace opens a door that leads into a separate wing of offices, then points to an empty office on the right. "This will belong to Hayes someday. He chose it as a child because he can see the water below."

The vision of a small Hayes running through this place warms me, and I glance at Jace. "He loves you, you know."

Jace's expression falters momentarily, his smile fading into a more serious, contemplative look. "I know. I don't make it easy for him."

I give him a playful shrug. "Not hitting on me might help."

A chuckle rumbles through his chest. "Noted."

We approach another secretary sitting at a desk perpendicular to a large office. The door is closed, but I can see through the windows on either side, which gives me a glimpse of the Boston skyline just outside.

"Cynthia," Andrew greets. "Frank in?"

"He is, but—"

I step past the secretary, barely acknowledging her, as I march into Frank Fitzgerald's office. She calls for me to stop and tells Andrew that Frank is on the phone, but a freight train wouldn't be able to stop me from speaking to this man.

Frank Fitzgerald's office is exactly what I expected: cold, sterile, and entirely devoid of warmth. The polished wood furniture, the expensive art on the walls, and the massive desk that seems to put him on a pedestal. I can feel the weight of his power and his control pressing down on me the second I step inside. But none of that matters. I came here with a single purpose and won't leave until I've clarified myself.

Frank Fitzgerald is sitting behind his desk, leaned back in his chair while talking to someone on the phone. He barely glances my way when I burst through his office door.

Jace and Andrew trail in behind me like two bodyguards.

"I assume you know why I'm here," I shout, my voice cold and unwavering.

Frank looks from me to Andrew to Jace, then mutters something to the person on the other end of the call and places the receiver down. "Andrew. Jace." His greeting is dry. "And I assume you're Fallon." He isn't actually asking. He knows exactly who I am. I hate how he looks at me—as if I'm just another obstacle in his plan, something to be dealt with quickly and efficiently.

I slam the grant check down onto his desk, the thick paper making a sharp sound as it lands. "I refuse to accept this," I say, my voice dripping with fury. "I'm here to tell you that I'm not taking a single dime from you or your company. I'm not going to be part of the scheme you've created to ruin your son's life."

Frank raises an eyebrow, unbothered by my outburst. He doesn't flinch. "I'm afraid I don't understand what you're talking about."

I don't let him get away with playing innocent. "Cut the bullshit, Frank. I know what's going on. You've set this entire thing up so that Hayes has to marry Raquel to keep her father from pushing you out of your precious business. You're too much of a coward to handle your own problems, so you've dragged your son into it."

I step closer to him, my hands clenched into fists by my sides. "You want to talk about sacrifice, Frank? Look at what you've done to him. You've asked him to marry someone he doesn't love just to save your skin, and you don't even have the decency to give him a choice in the matter. How fucking lucky you are to still have your family intact while you've completely destroyed your son's chance at happiness. You've put his whole future on the line so that you can keep your power. You're an ass."

Frank's face darkens, but I don't care. I'm not afraid of him. And looking at him, I'm not sure why everyone else is either. "You don't understand the magnitude of the situation, Fallon," he says, his tone low and threatening. "This isn't just about Hayes. It's about the future of this company and the livelihoods of the people who depend on it. I didn't make the rules. I'm doing what I have to do to secure our legacy."

I laugh bitterly. "Secure your legacy? Is that what you're calling it? You're not securing anything. You're just a man too afraid to stand up to Raquel's father, so you're sacrificing your son to protect your pride." I fold my arms over my chest and shrug. "If you were actually decent at your job, you wouldn't be so afraid of losing control. If you were good at what you do, you wouldn't have to manipulate your son into marrying someone just to keep the business from slipping through your fingers."

My eyes narrow with uncontained rage. "You're a coward. A selfish, power-hungry coward. And I will not be part of this. I won't take your grant money, and I won't let you use me to keep your son trapped in this mess. If you want to fight for control, come at me with everything you've got. Because I'm not going anywhere. I won't let you destroy him like this. I won't let Hayes sacrifice his future just because you're too weak. You might be fooling everyone else but you're not fooling me. There's something you're scared of."

Frank's jaw tightens, his fists clenching on the armrests of his chair, but he says nothing. He doesn't need to. The tension in the air is thick, and I feel the gravity of the moment. I'm not going to walk away from this. Not when it's about Hayes. I won't let Hayes sacrifice his happiness and future to satisfy Frank's ego.

"You think you can just walk away from all of this?" Frank asks; his voice is quieter now but still full of contempt. "You think you can make demands when you're not even part of this family?"

I stand straighter, feeling the weight of my decision settling over me like a shield. "I'm not part of your family, Frank. And that's the point. I'm not going to be your pawn. I won't let you use me as leverage to get what you want. If you think I'll just sit back and let you manipulate every-thing, you're wrong."

His eyes burn with anger, but I don't flinch. I've made my decision, and I won't back down.

I turn, heading for the door without a second glance, but Andrew stops me with a gentle touch on my arm. "Wait," he says, looking directly at Frank. "I quit. I've spent years watching you tear down Hayes when all he's ever wanted was a little respect from his father. I won't be part of it anymore."

Jace's parting goodbye is to flip Frank off with both middle fingers, slipping a bottle of whiskey from his alcohol cart before following me and Andrew out.

I hook my arm through Andrew's. "Take me to Fitz. I assume you two know where he is."

"Thanks to me," Jace says proudly, slipping his phone out while taking a sip of liquor.

I expected Andrew to have paled or regret his decision about quitting, but I've never seen him so relaxed. "I'm proud of you," I say.

"I only stayed for Hayes," Andrew explains, pressing the elevator button. "Being here has always been his dream, but only because he wasn't allowed to want anything different."

Jace tells us his location as we step onto the elevator, then adds, "I believe it's time we change that."

And for the first time, I agree with him.

*hayes*

I'm trying to focus. Really, I am. But everything about tonight is wrong.

The restaurant is luxurious, of course, but it feels suffocating tonight. The heavy linen tablecloth, the delicate glassware, and the dim lighting all feel like a theater set, and I'm stuck playing a role I don't want. My back is straight, my tie perfectly adjusted, and my smile rehearsed. And across the table from me sits Raquel, a glass of sparkling water delicately held in her slender fingers, her face lit by the warm glow of the candle between us.

It should be a night to discuss the plans about the wedding, the details, and our the future. But... all I can think about is Fallon. I can't stop seeing the way her eyes looked when I confessed, and how my heart twisted when I realized what I would lose. The weight of everything I'm about to give up is gnawing at me.

Raquel's voice pulls me from my thoughts. "Hayes," she says, her tone cool but familiar. "Are you listening?"

I blink, focusing on her for the first time in a while. She's talking about the wedding, of course. Or about the dress, the venue, the date... I lost myself in thoughts of

Fallon around the time the waiter brought the drinks. "Yeah, sorry," I mutter, taking a sip of my wine to steady myself. "I was just... lost in thought."

Raquel tilts her head, studying me. She's always been perceptive, even when I didn't want her to be. Aside from the disaster we were while sleeping together, she's always been a friend. She knows me well. Similar to Andrew and Jace, Raquel grew up with me. The four of us know everything about each other and our families. It's a price we've paid to have allies.

"What's bothering you?" she asks, a small frown pulling at the corners of her lips. "You've been distant all night."

I force a smile, though it feels more like a grimace. "It's nothing, really. Just a lot on my mind."

She doesn't buy it. "It's the girl from the banquet, isn't it?"

I freeze. My heart thuds painfully in my chest as I meet her sharp and probing gaze. She has always read me like a book, and I've never been good at lying to her. But the truth... The truth feels like an anchor around my neck, and I can't bring myself to admit it. Even as I take a drink to avoid answering, my mouth feels like it's full of sand.

Raquel's lips part, her voice softening. "You're in love with her, aren't you?"

Raquel's empathy is tangible, her understanding of my struggle evident in her eyes. Her compassion is a balm to my aching heart. I look down at my hands, unable to meet her eyes. "I... I didn't mean for it to happen," I admit quietly, my voice barely above a whisper. "I fell in love with her so quickly. It shocked me. It really did. I didn't want it. Fuck, I didn't even think it was possible for me to fall in love with the way my parents are. But when I look at her... I feel something I've never felt before. Something real."

Raquel is quiet for a long moment, and when she finally speaks, her tone is calm, almost resigned. "Life's too short to live without that, Hayes. I won't be part of you not being with the person you love. You should go after her if she means that much to you."

I blink, completely stunned by her sudden change of heart. "What are you saying?"

Raquel takes a deep breath, pushing her glass away, her fingers trembling slightly as she wipes her palms on her napkin. "We've been living for our fathers our entire lives, Fitz." She places her hand over mine. "It's time to stop."

My brow furrows. "But what about you? I know your father about as well as I know mine—"

"It'll be fine," she says, cutting me off before I can finish. Her eyes flicker, a small, almost imperceptible sadness crossing her features, but she quickly masks it with a smile. "I don't need to keep playing this part, Hayes. I never wanted to marry you, but I understood why it had to happen. But I won't be the reason why you don't fight for what you want. I won't be the reason you spend the rest of your life hating yourself for not being with the person you love."

I sit here, stunned into silence. Everything she's saying is unraveling my entire plan, the walls I've built around myself to protect me from falling apart. I wasn't prepared for this, for her understanding… especially not for her kindness. "You're willing to do this for me? Why would you even approach my father with a threat then?" I whisper, the disbelief in my voice impossible to hide.

Raquel blinks rapidly, confusion knitted in her brow. "Me? I wasn't the one to threaten anyone, Hayes. He was." She leans in closer, lowering her voice. "I did approach him about the pregnancy because I needed advice from someone who knows my father well, but he was the one who threatened to tell him. He said he'd help me by claiming you're the father, but only if I marry you."

I stare at her, the words sinking in slowly. The weight

of it all is staggering. "Wait, what? He called me into his office and said you were the one to threaten him—that you'd tell your father the baby is mine and that I walked away from you."

We stare at one another in silence for a long moment. Neither of us stand to gain anything by lying to one another now. We've both been lied to by my father, but why? Why would he go to such lengths to please Raquel's father? "He's hiding something," I say slowly, mind racing. "But I haven't been involved enough to know what it could be."

Raquel's annoyance is evident. She's realizing she was tricked into this, too. We almost gave away our entire futures because of something my father is trying to cover. "Whatever it is, it's big enough for him to try and cover his ass. And I'm going to find out what it is, Hayes. If I do, if I uncover it—"

"I know," I interrupt. "He could be pushed out. I wouldn't ever be part of FFJ." I expect disappointment or fear to follow that realization, but all I feel is relief when I utter those words aloud. And all I see front and center in my mind is Fallon. She's my future.

She is all that matters.

This is my chance to walk away. Now is the time to free myself from the chains of my father's expectations. The gravity of this decision, the enormity of the choice before me, is almost suffocating.

"I'll help you in any way I can." I toss my napkin down on the table. "I've always tried to do what's right for my family, but I'm done now. We can take him down together."

She raises her glass, waiting for me to tap mine against hers. "I have someone I can talk to that might be able to look into his emails. Frank is smart, Hayes. This won't be simple."

She's referring to Jace's father. He was the first one I thought of, too.

"Everyone has a weakness. We just need to find his." I release a deep breath. "I'm sorry you were brought into this. I should've just talked to you about it, but I'm learning my communication needs a little work."

"More than a little," she says with a genuine smile. "But I understand more than anyone why you didn't question him. Now, go. Go find Fallon, Hayes. I'll call you tomorrow."

"Thank you," I say, my voice thick with emotion. "I won't abandon you, Raquel."

"Don't look back, Hayes. Not for a second."

The weight on my shoulders lifts. I feel like I can breathe again for the first time in a long time. I push back my chair, standing up quickly, my pulse racing with the urgency of everything that just happened.

As I weave through the restaurant, I try to push aside the lingering doubts, the fear that I've just made a mistake. But there's no time for second-guessing.

I need to find Fallon.

---

I walk out onto the sidewalk, the night air biting at my skin as I rush toward the street. The city feels so empty without her, and my heart aches with every step I take. She could still be in Missouri, which means it'll be hours before I see her again. I'll need a private plane…

I stop short when I see them. Fallon, Andrew, and Jace are standing by the curb, talking in hushed voices. When they see me, Andrew and Jace step back while avoiding eye-contact with me, leaving Fallon standing there alone. Aside from the ravishing creature before me, the other two are complete idiots. "If you hadn't brought her with you,

I'd be disabling my tracking," I tell them, then refocus on Fallon. "What are you doing here?" I ask, my voice hoarse.

She confidently strolls toward me. "I know everything. About the marriage. The contract. The grant. The sacrifices you made. I know what you were willing to do to protect me from your father's wrath." She's less than a foot away from me now, her chin tipped up defiantly. "But I've handled it. I've told your father to come at me with all he's got. I'm not running. I'm not going anywhere."

I stand frozen, my eyes wide, disbelief and relief fighting for dominance in my gaze. "Fallon…" I say her name like a prayer. But my face twists with concern. "I never wanted you to know all of this. I wanted to protect you from it. I didn't want you to have to carry any of this weight to understand how deep it runs. It's not just me, Fallon. It's everything. Everything I've been forced to carry my entire life. And I wanted you to be free of it."

"I know," she says softly as she reaches up to cup my face. "I know all of it, Hayes. But we can't carry this weight separately anymore. Not when I've always felt so much for you and still do."

My breathing hitches, my jaw tightening as I search her eyes for some flicker of truth. "Fallon, I don't know what to do with all of this. I never wanted to hurt you. I never wanted to drag you into this… this mess of my family, my obligations. I didn't want you to have to choose between me and your dreams."

She shakes her head, her fingers tracing the sharp lines of my jaw. My heart races. I'm so deeply in love with this girl that I feel I might melt into her touch.

"You don't get it, Fitz," she whispers, her voice thick with emotion. "I never *had* to choose. Not between you and my dreams. Because when I'm with you, I feel like I'm whole. Like I'm finally not carrying everything alone."

My hands find her waist, pulling her just a little closer.

"You don't know how hard this is for me," I murmur. "I'm supposed to protect you, Fallon." I rest my forehead against hers, and I can feel the beat of her heart racing in time with mine. The distance between us has melted away, and now there is nothing but the two of us standing in the heart of a storm we haven't yet learned to navigate together.

"Fitz," she breathes, pulling back just slightly so I can see the vulnerability in her eyes. "I love you."

The words hang in the air for a beat, both of us holding onto them like they're the only truth that matters. My lips part, and I see the raw emotion flash in her eyes before I crush her against me, my lips crashing onto hers.

The kiss is desperate and hungry. It's a kiss that speaks of weeks of yearning, unspoken promises, and hearts long locked behind too many walls. My hands tangle in her hair, pulling her impossibly closer as if I can make up for all the lost time with the heat of this kiss. She responds just as fiercely, her hands tracing the lines of my back, feeling the tension built between us for so long melt away in the intensity of the moment.

It isn't just a kiss—it's everything. Every unsaid word, every bit of hurt, every piece of longing that had built between us like a wall is finally being torn down, brick by brick. The kiss deepens, slow and passionate, and for a moment, I can taste my regret and her hope, everything we've kept buried under layers of guilt and responsibility.

When we finally break apart, both of us breathless, I can barely register the racing thoughts in my head. I'm unsure where we go from here, but the one thing I know for sure is that I'm not going to walk away.

Not now. Not ever.

"I love you too," I whisper against her lips, my voice thick with emotion. "I've loved you from the moment I met you. And I'm so sorry it took me this long to admit it."

I wanted to say it first. I should've said it first. But like always, Fallon didn't hesitate to tell me how she feels. Someday, I hope to be as forthcoming with how I feel about her as she has been with me. "You inspire me to be better every day, my little tragedy."

She smiles through tears, her hand gently cupping my face, my thumb brushing over her cheekbone. "It's not too late," she says softly. "We can still make it. We can fight this. Together."

My chest rises and falls rapidly with every breath, and I can see the hesitation in her eyes and the fear of the unknown, but it isn't enough to make her pull away.

"I don't know what comes next," I say, my voice ragged, "but I know one thing for sure: I can't imagine my life without you in it."

"We'll make it work," she whispers. "No more secrets. No more running. We're in this together."

My lips brush hers again, tender and sweet this time. I just want to savor this moment. She clings to me, knowing that this is just the beginning of a new chapter for both of us.

But as I pull away, the weight of our situation returns. I lock eyes with Andrew, his hesitation mirroring mine. This is far from over. We both know that the battle isn't over yet. Frank will never give up. He'll come for me, come for our entire future. But for the first time, I don't feel afraid. I don't feel like I'm carrying this alone.

Fallon is with me now.

And I won't let anything tear us apart.

*note*

Follow Whitney on Instagram for future bonus content and announcements featuring Fallon and Hayes, including their fight against Frank Fitzgerald and what lies ahead.

Instagram: whitneydeanwrites

# *acknowledgments*

I sit on a plane, sighing at the absurd amount of times the woman sitting in the seat in front of me is adjusting and shaking my laptop, and I think about each person on this flight. I write stories to sustain my life, but their lives are their stories. Much of my life has been spent as an observer —one of the hazards of being an empath, I suppose. And I rarely stop to think about my own story; the one I'm supposed to be writing. Instead, I put pieces of me into every story I write, clawing my way through obscure, buried parts of myself.

I always run from the problems I don't want to solve, searching for a feeling in a different place. But even I don't know which feeling I'm yearning for. Is it feeling free from the choices I've made that have led me to where I am? (sitting on yet another flight, already dreading returning home.) Because if I sit still in one place for too long, the noises become too loud, too stimulating: I begin feeling trapped in a room full of people because they're writing their stories while I'm sprinting from mine. And time has always felt like an enemy.

Or are we all just masks sketched onto a page? And maybe it's the panic of each interaction I have slowly erasing the facade I've spent so long crafting that keeps me moving. Perhaps it's the search of finding someone who can break down the walls that keeps me climbing.

*Rest,* they'd say, *breathe.*

How can the willingness to grow and evolve be coupled with such crippling fear and regret?

*Just pick up the pen,* I tell myself as I slowly board another flight, but the ink is invisible and I bleed onto the page.

Xoxo,
  Whitney